AMBUSHED!

Soaked in sweat and dust, Slocum drew his hand carefully to wipe clear his vision. In the next instant, he knew exactly where his attacker was.

He would have given plenty for the Winchester that was only a few yards away in the saddleboot.

The movement was slight, as innocent as a whisper of air; only it wasn't air. Swifter than thought, Slocum's finger squeezed. A string of oaths mixed with a cry of pain, and the bushwhacker's bullet tore into the sky as his rifle clattered to the stony ground.

John Slocum's words were as hard as the spent bullet.

"On your feet and stretch it!"

* * *

SPECIAL PREVIEW!

Turn to the back of this book for an exciting look at a new epic trilogy . . .

NORTHWEST DESTINY

. . . the sprawling saga of brotherhood, pride and rage on the American frontier.

DON'T MISS THESE
ALL-ACTION WESTERN SERIES
FROM THE BERKLEY PUBLISHING GROUP

THE GUNSMITH by J. R. Roberts
Clint Adams was a legend among lawmen, outlaws, and ladies. They called him . . . the Gunsmith.

LONGARM by Tabor Evans
The popular long-running series about U.S. Deputy Marshal Long—his life, his loves, his fight for justice.

LONE STAR by Wesley Ellis
The blazing adventures of Jessica Starbuck and the martial arts master, Ki. Over eight million copies in print.

SLOCUM by Jake Logan
Today's longest-running action western. John Slocum rides a deadly trail of hot blood and cold steel.

JAKE LOGAN

SLOCUM AND THE BUSHWHACKERS

BERKLEY BOOKS, NEW YORK

SLOCUM AND THE BUSHWHACKERS

A Berkley Book / published by arrangement with
the author

PRINTING HISTORY
Berkley edition / September 1992

ISBN: 0-425-13401-6

A BERKLEY BOOK® TM 757,375
Berkley Books are published by The Berkley Publishing Group,
200 Madison Avenue, New York, New York 10016.
The name "BERKLEY" and the "B" logo
are trademarks belonging to Berkley Publishing Corporation.

PRINTED IN THE UNITED STATES OF AMERICA

10 9 8 7 6 5 4 3 2 1

SLOCUM AND THE BUSHWHACKERS

1

Lucky!

The crack of the Henry rifle was still echoing off the rimrocks as John Slocum hit hardpan. Even before the impact he was rolling, scrambling, diving into the meager protection of a clump of sage, a lone rock, knuckles scraping as he yanked the Colt .44 from its leather holster.

There wasn't even time to cuss before the second bullet spanked a stone only inches from his face, whining off into the long blue sky.

In the moments between shots he'd spied a larger rock, and now he was inching, almost swimming on the bone-hard ground, his hands, feet, eyes, his very urgency pulling him to safety. At least for the moment. But he was a big man whose broad shoulders weren't easy to conceal.

Soaked in sweat and dust, he drew his hand carefully to wipe clear his vision, now noting the smear of blood on his knuckles. Then, in the next instant, he knew exactly where the man was.

In the abrupt silence he listened to the ticking heat, his breath sounding to him like a pump. A jay called suddenly, and he wondered if there was more than one rifle trying for him. Then he saw the bird lifting from the wide bush just in front of the line of spruce that edged the stand of high timber. He would have given more than plenty for the Winchester that was only a few yards away in his saddleboot. His Appaloosa stood still, his ears up, nostrils blowing a little, then dropped his head to snort at the ground, looking for feed that wasn't there.

But the horse knew where the man with the rifle was; Slocum watched him, now spotting the jay that swept in to land close to the bullberry bush, but changed its mind and veered off. He was sure now that there was only one bushwhacker. The Appaloosa had his ears forward and up, and now Slocum brought his Colt right in line with his bead on the bushwhacker.

The movement was as slight, as innocent as a whisper of air, only it wasn't air. Swifter than thought, Slocum's finger squeezed. A string of oaths mixed with a cry of pain, and the bushwhacker's bullet tore into the sky as his rifle clattered to the stony ground.

John Slocum's words were as hard as the spent bullet.

"On your feet and stretch it!"

"Awright . . . All *right*!"

An extraordinary figure rose from behind the bush, arms stretched high almost in exaggeration of the traditional posture of surrender.

Slocum was also on his feet, waiting, listening to even the vibration of the would-be killer's movement, the Colt pointing right at the belly of his prisoner.

"You alone?"

"What the fuck's it look like, fer Chrissakes! No, I ain't alone; I got the United States Cavalry with me!"

The voice sounded like a half dozen files being rubbed across a gun barrel.

Slocum did not pick up on the salty humor; he was noticing something more than the dumpy pants held up by dirty yellow galluses, the dull red and black hickory shirt, the chewed-up Stetson pulled down almost on top of those dark eyes that looked like a pair of malevolent bullets. It was something else . . .

"Why did you shoot at me?" he demanded.

"On account of I love ya, you dumb shit!" The voice crackled with anger. "What you doin' on DV Range, huh? Mister!" Now the head bent forward out of the hunched shoulders, and from that surly mouth shot a streak of saliva.

Holy Moses, Slocum thought, recollecting the old woman he'd come upon after a wagon train rubout down by South Pass two winters ago. It wasn't her, but that type for sure. And yet the memory was more than that. Something else rang a bell.

"Don't know what you're talkin' about, M'am. I'm just riding through, and I have got no notion whose range is whose. Myself, I always figured the range was free country. 'Course . . ." He shrugged.

His prisoner was more than equal to the occasion, however. "You listen to me, Mister smart alec!

This here is DV Range. I am VanDam; this here is my outfit—DV Range, see—an' I don't want any Bart Gooden scum riding about with his nose all over the place!" She sniffed wetly, hawked, and spat. "Now skin yer ass off. I don't give a shit how much gun you got on me!"

At this point Slocum couldn't control himself any longer and he burst into a loud laugh. "Well, by damn if I don't remember Dolores—Dolly Dolores VanDam, by golly!"

"Where'd you hear of me!" The words shot at him like a striking snake.

"Well," he said easily, holstering the six-gun. "I don't believe it was in church. Lemme see . . . Got it! K.C. it was. Annie Chambers's place . . ." He stood there grinning at her while her face darkened.

"Never heard of such a place! Yer lyin' like a rope, but that's to be expected."

But he knew he'd hit.

"Never seen you before this day, mister. What's yer handle, anyways?"

"Slocum. John Slocum."

The hat brim tilted back so that the hard eyes could take a closer look.

"Heard of you. Can't remember where, but I heard the name."

And suddenly Slocum caught a different voice behind all that stuffed clothing and anger, not so raspy, not so hard. Yes—younger was it? The fleeting memory, passing so quickly he almost wondered if maybe he'd imagined it. Except he knew he hadn't. He knew it was there. He knew that person was more than just pockets and patches and whatever else was binding an anger he knew he didn't want to mess with. Though he would if he had to.

"I am telling you I never heard of any Bart Gooden," he said now. "I am just riding through."

"Mister, you don't look to me like the type to be riding the grubline. And not from what I have heard anyways. You sure your name is Slocum? *the* John Slocum?" The malevolence had returned to the grainy voice, the bronze eyes.

"The name is not *the* John Slocum, just John Slocum," he said, and his voice was not soft. "Just Slocum will do."

A beat, and then, "Handy with a gun, I bin told."

"Now and again somebody gets in the way of it."

"Huh!"

"You got off lucky."

"Huh . . ." She had lifted her hand to her chin, and he now saw the strip of blood where his bullet had grazed her cheek.

"You got any jawbreaker back at the outfit?" And when he caught her hesitation he said sourly, "I'll split up some firewood so's you won't feel put out."

They walked to the edge of the stand of trees where a little steel-dust gelding with a low-canteled saddle stood ground-hitched. Right away he saw by the way she handled him that she knew her horseflesh.

When he mounted his Appaloosa he looked at her and said, "Well . . . ?"

He saw something that looked almost like a grin appearing through the shadow thrown by the wide hatbrim, but it didn't get much further than a suggestion.

"Had a choreboy a while back," she said, talking to the horizon now, "That sonofabitch Bart Gooden run his ass off the place. Gun-dancing the poor old bugger with his Winchester from quite some distance off."

"Clever, huh," said Slocum.

"Wasn't all that far away, but that man Gooden is for sure accurate with a weapon. And he don't give a damn who he shoots or where or when or how. He is a devil, and that's a gut!"

"What about that arbuckle?" Slocum said. "I am not aimin' to hire on as your choreboy, but I will pay for it." And then he added, "Providin' it don't taste too much like axle grease . . ." And he added respectfully, not batting an eye, "Ma'am."

The DV Range wasn't far from where the confrontation with its owner had taken place, but the trail across the top of the rimrocks made slow going. They rode in silence, and Slocum had plenty of time to size up his situation.

Obviously he'd dropped into the middle of a trouble it would be best to avoid. He'd already had plenty to handle in eluding the self-appointed vigilantes back in Rabbit Rock who had suddenly decided that they could enforce their authority in that part of the country by stringing up a few designated trouble-making citizens. Not that Slocum had caused any trouble, other than taking pains to avoid being bullied by the Simmers gang into attempting to outdraw a half dozen of the so-called vigilantes under the command of the self-appointed Captain

Simmers. He'd declined the invitation and had gotten clean away, only to nearly come a cropper with Dolly Dolores VanDam. Well, trouble often came in company with more trouble, he knew. Maybe there was something more waiting for him.

The trail was narrow and rough, but Slocum's tough little Appaloosa was sure-footed and had been well-broken by the half-breed who'd sold him. He was glad for the quiet ride, glad to take in the silence. It was what he liked best about the Rockies—the big silence, the listening in which a man could find himself again. The silence was always there when you turned to it.

Following the stubby steel-dust gelding as they picked their way across the rimrocks, he was pleased to see how his companion kept away from the skyline. Dolly Dolores was no dumbbell, not about the cards, he knew, and clearly not about riding the country. He figured she knew men, too—to the bone. And yet, she had a face that could stand a good chance of stopping a charging Brahma steer. Crazy! Still, there was something about her he didn't mind admitting that he liked. Well, she clearly would need all she had in the face of what seemed to be going on. Range trouble was no easy riding.

It was windy the way it often is in the mountains of Wyoming, with the sky clear as an echo. Relaxing his eyes for better vision, he took in the sweep of the great valley that ran all the way to Hardtown, which he knew from the grubline talk was a string of hamlets housing a couple of thousand people. It sat in the middle of the valley, on the western bank of the Sawbuck River, the land sweeping up the long slopes to the high tips of the Buffalo Range. Cattle grazed on the great brown and green patches and he could see horses and a half dozen log houses and their outbuildings making up that many ranches.

Presently, they rode into a stand of tall timber—pine, spruce, and fir. Good building logs, Slocum noted, tall, straight, and even for almost the whole length, between eight and ten inches in diameter. They broke through to a clearing and looked down at what he figured had to be the DV outfit—three log cabins and a barn. At the same time he realized that he was not only right in the center of the cattle country thereabouts, but also in the center of trouble.

"There she is." Dolly Dolores drew rein, and they sat their ponies, studying the thin spiral of smoke lifting from the chimney of the larger cabin.

"You've got no help?" Slocum observed, making it a question so as not to offend her, though he'd noticed no horses in the corral, but more especially the fact that the place just looked like it was short of hands.

"Had two hands—fair-to-middlin'—till that son-ofabitch Bart run 'em off. Goddam chickens!"

"Somebody's built that fire," Slocum observed.

"That is what I know," his companion said drily.

They shared the silence for another moment and then Slocum said, "Those other outfits. Yonder across the river, and the two we rode by."

"That's Casper Flint th'other side of the Saw-buck." The beaten-up Stetson nodded toward the river. "Them other two, the one with the big hoss corral where you seen somebody sackin' a bronc. That was Wendell Cole's. And the outfit we just come by with the wagon box out front, that was Torgerson's."

"And where is this feller Bart? He got an outfit? Or does he hire out?"

"Both. There's a place called Prairie Dog around the base of Carter Mountain yonder." She nodded toward a mountain that rose steeply on the other side of the river. "His outfit's in one of them canyons, I bin told. Never been there. Damn few bin there, I have heard. Though I bin invited." And she looked wryly at him.

"Hmm." He studied it a moment and then he asked again, "Gooden works for himself or somebody else?"

"Nobody 'pears to know."

"Maybe both, huh?"

"Maybe both. That man is all sonofabitch and a yard wide."

"I figured that already," Slocum said drily.

"One of these days I am going to get that bastard's balls in a block 'n takle an' string him to the top of one of them pine trees. Leave the sonofabitch there as a warning to rustlers, hoss thieves, brand switchers—the whole fuckin' bunch of ne'er-do-wells."

The Appaloosa suddenly bobbed his head to get rid of a couple of deer flies, and snorted.

"Man 'pears to be dead set on yerself, seems to me," Slocum said slyly, looking to get a rise out of her.

"That's on account of he's been tryin' to cut in on my business and I keep hazin' him off."

Slocum looked at her squarely then, taking in the even features, the slightly pug nose, the wide-set burnished eyes, and the dark brown hair that seemed to have been pushed under the Stetson after it was on her head.

"What kind of business are you talking about?"

"Jesus . . ." said the lady under the battered hat.

Slocum made no reply, but shifted his big body, the saddle leather creaking while his pony took a small step to even his balance.

They quartered down the long slope toward the log buildings, with Slocum letting his hostess take the lead. The surprise took only a moment to settle; he'd already half-suspected something of that nature. And he thought, why not? Why keep all the business in town. Why not bring it into the country. After all, it was a much needed service.

All the same, an interesting surprise. Yet the surprise that greeted him when he walked into the cabin behind Dolly Dolores made it all appear quite pale.

It was in the way she turned from the stove. Entering the kitchen after Dolly Dolores, he had seen only a back, for she was poking the range into further action, and the flame was shooting up.

"Brought a visitor," Dolly said, her voice bland with remembered hostility and caution.

"So I see."

Slocum had shut the door behind him. The girl at the stove was wearing a blue and white calico dress with white trimming at the neck and cuffs. She looked at him. She had managed to turn from her work swiftly, yet without haste. There was a grace in her movement that caught him—plus the fact that she was beautiful. Just the right height. Brown hair, brown eyes out of which a sense of humor regarded him calmly.

There was a hint of pleased laughter in her voice as she said, "How do you do."

Slocum felt it run all the way through him.

But the moment was fleeting. Their companion's voice fell into the room with all the sociability of a barbed-wire fence. "You don't have to stare a hole in her, mister. It's just my kid sister, and I'm letting you know right now she ain't a part of what we was talking about."

"I'm Sally."

"Pleased to meet you, Miss VanDam."

"Sally McQuarie."

"She's adopted," Dolly Dolores broke in. "Got a different handle."

"Can we offer you some coffee, sir?" Turning to her sister with amusement dancing in her large brown eyes, "Dolly, dear, won't you introduce the gentleman?"

Slocum, slightly paralyzed as a result of his surprise and delight, started to speak, but the figure, under the big, battered Stetson barked out, "Figgered the two of you got yourselves sized up pretty directly without me helpin'. This here is Slocum. John Slocum. So he claims," Dolly Dolores added with a rancid look at the guest. "He is needin' coffee."

The girl was looking at him quizzically, her lips just slightly parted, and Slocum felt a surge of passion racing all through him. He had no doubt the feeling was reciprocated.

"Have a chair, sir." She turned toward Dolly. "Or maybe in the front room?"

"Don't make no difference." Dolly's eyes were on Slocum, probing. "You can throw yer duffle in the bunkhouse if you've a mind to. You'll get supper, and you can do chores to pay for it 'less you got money."

"Dolly!" Her sister had lifted the stove lid and was poking at the fire. "That's not the way to treat a guest."

"Listen, this here feller damn near blew my head off with his handgun!"

But Slocum stepped in swiftly. "Miss, I appreciate the hospitality, but I really ought to be riding on to Hardtown."

"Suit yerself," Dolly Dolores cut in, swift as a knife. "But you might like to sample the merchandise. That's the further log house, nearest the crick."

Slocum was looking at Sally McQuarie.

Dolly's next words drove into him like bullets. "My sister is *not* part of that there. I do believe I told you."

The girl had turned from the stove, still holding the lid, and was just starting to protest, but Slocum was quicker.

"I was just wondering if your sister spoke French?" he said, innocent as a dove.

"Jesus!" Dolly Dolores's eyes were studying his face as though trying to probe the mystery of creation. "What the hell does that mean!"

Sally had thrown back her head and was shaking with laughter. "Doll, I am very happy to meet Mister Slocum. He is a much needed addition to the boring life of the Great Frontier."

Her eyes met Slocum's then. "No, I am not part of the merchandise, as my sister so quaintly put it, and I know that you were not thinking I was, sir." And all at once she blushed. She turned quickly away, reaching for the pot on the stove. "Why don't you both sit. This is silly. Oh, and I am sorry. I do not speak French." And her eyes crinkled again with laughter.

Slocum stepped forward quickly, reaching for the pot. "Let me help you, miss." And without intention his hand brushed hers as they both reached for the coffee.

"After you, miss." He stepped back.

"Please have a seat."

In another moment they were seated at the table in the front room. Sally had brought a plate of baking powder biscuits.

"You see, we knew a visitor was coming," she said. "They're fresh this morning."

"They're still plenty fresh," he said, joining her camaraderie with a grin.

"And there's jam in that," she said, pointing to a jar.

Dolly, her mouth crammed with biscuit, lifted her cup and began to speak. "Slocum here says he never heard of Bart Gooden. Don't know whether to believe him or not. Anyways, I like to shot him with that old Henry. That is the poorest excuse for a weapon I ever come across."

"Tell me something about this man Gooden," Slocum said. "You say his first name is *Bart*?" He underlined the word as though trying to recollect something.

"Yup." Dolly Dolores nodded, and then took a gurgling swig from her cup of coffee.

"Doll . . ."

"My kid sister's still tryin' to bring me up like a lady, fer Chrissakes! What do you think of that!" And bringing her cup down with a bang on the hard table she glared first at Sally, then at Slocum.

"I think it don't hurt to know how to do everythin'," Slocum said, drawling the words extra slow.

This brought a robust chuckle from Dolly and a smile from her sister.

Then he said, "Tell me what this Bart looks like. Short? Heavyset? A big head? Got a scar under his left eye?"

Dolly was staring at him. "Said you didn't know him!"

"I said I didn't know Bart Gooden. The man I just described is—or at least *was*—named Bart Rankin."

"Himself," Dolly said, sitting back in her chair and pursing her lips. "The sonofabitch. Where and how do you know him?"

"Dolly, calm down. Mister Slocum is our guest, and you're talking to him as though you're about to arrest him."

"Trust nobody but yerself, my girl, then you'll know who done you the dirty!"

Slocum had suddenly lifted his hand for quiet. "You expecting company?"

"Nope." Dolly's big head started to wag but stopped, as she froze, listening.

"What about your business?" And he nodded toward the creek.

"Could be. But I wouldn't say likely. There is roundup."

"It also could be something else," Slocum said.

"That's what I know."

The horses were coming in fast. Dolly got up and walked into the kitchen to peer through one of the windows. "They're coming in like they mean business. I don't figure it's a pleasure visit."

"Is it Gooden?"

"Don't look like him. Likely some of his hands."

Slocum cut a fast look at the girl who was calmly clearing the table. "I'll handle this," he said to the figure standing beside the window, out of view of anyone outside trying to see in.

"It ain't your business, mister."

Slocum had stepped close to have a look. "I count six," he said. "They look like customers to you?"

"Not the kind I want. But there is a way to find out." And she started to the door.

"Dolly, be careful! Why not wait a minute and see." The alarm in Sally's voice rang through the cabin.

The riders were right there in front of the window, pulling up in a thin sheet of dust.

"Six, huh!" Dolly sniffed. "Horny as hell or drunk, I've no doubt. Or the both."

"How many girls do you have?" Slocum asked.

"Three right now," Dolly turned swiftly. "Sal, you stay right out of sight!"

"I wasn't thinking of inviting them in, my dear sister."

Slocum caught the irritation in her voice, and felt the alarm in Dolly's. But his main attention was with the visitors who were not dismounting.

And then one of them called out. "Hey, Dolly! We got a message for ya!"

"That sonofabitch! I can guess what it is," Dolly snapped, stepping toward the door of the cabin with the Henry in one hand.

"I'll handle this," Slocum said firmly. "Owe you for the coffee and that fine biscuit," he added swiftly to forestall objections from the women, and before either of them could say anything he opened the door and stepped outside to face the six horsemen. He was feeling a sudden question in his mind as the cool mountain air hit his face and hands.

From behind him came the gravelly admonition. "Take it slow. Slocum. I got you covered."

All six were still mounted. Their guns were holstered, though within easy reach. For a moment he'd thought they might be a posse from Rabbit Rock, but there were too many of them; they wouldn't have sent a whole half dozen riders when a lone bushwhacker could have done the job.

Even so, he didn't lose any of his caution. That special sense that was so often with him told that there had to be something extra. It was too neat, because they were obviously bringing a message. He heard his Appaloosa nicker then and saw him standing in the round horse corral. He watched the horse shake his head and mane at some deer flies, then he dropped his head to lick at the salt block lying just inside the corral gate. But if it was a message they were bringing, then why six when two or even one could have done the job?

2

The three hunkered just inside the rim of the trees well back from the high ledge. Behind them their horses were ground-hitched, out of sight of anyone who might take it in mind to view that particular area on the side of the mountain.

"What you see, Coke?" the shortest of the three asked, his words mumbling and whistling past his hare lip. Yet, his companions had no trouble hearing him. They were used to him. However Coke, the thin man looking through field glasses, made no reply.

After a pause, the third man spoke. "See 'em now! That dust has gotta be the boys." He was a hard, heavy man wearing a black shirt, and his face was red where it wasn't covered by the tight black beard and trimmed black mustache. A scar beneath his left eye emphasized his obvious power. All round, the man was compact, muscled, looking as though his black shirt was pasted to his hard, rough, skin.

Some people made the mistake of thinking Bart

Gooden was all muscle and no brain, but they were apt to discover that summation to be faulty. Bart was all muscle, but not between the ears. He'd been a professional bareknuckler, yet now, retired from the squared circle, he earned his living not with his fists but with his gun, with guile, with brain as well as brawn. And he was—everyone said it— swift as a whistle with both handguns tied down on his lean hips. He had very long, thick fingernails, black with dirt, that he used to good advantage in a hand-to-hand fight.

Harelip Finn Thoms fully appreciated his associate's professionalism with those guns. He'd seen him light a lucifer match stuck on a corral pole with a single draw and shoot. It had not been luck, though the thought had since occurred to Harelip, but he had no mind to test it. No sir, he knew Bart Gooden was all everybody said he was, and probably more.

Coke Millers had started to lower his glasses, still keeping his eyes on the scene at the DV Range below where Hendry and the boys were bracing the man who'd just stepped out of the cabin.

"There's somebody there." Coke started to say, and before he could get to his next word, Bart Gooden whipped the field glasses out of his hand, scratching Coke's knuckle as he did so.

Coke looked down at the thin red line of blood as he fought to control his anger. He succeeded. Once, some while back, he'd not managed it, and even before he'd said a word, Bart had slammed him right smack on his ear, knocking him across a campfire and damn near settin' fire to his britches. The sonofabitch . . .

He glared now at the big man with that head built like a rock, his sudden anger pounding in his ears.

Still, Coke Millers was no coward. "Whyn't you say you wanted them glasses, fer Chrissakes! Them nails of yourn' like a fuckin' blade!"

"How come I keep 'em that way," Gooden said, real smug, his eyes not leaving the VanDam spread. "Who'd you reckon that sonofabitch down yonder is?" he said, his voice tight with irritation. "That dumb bitch! Don't tell me she's gone an' took on some new help."

Harelip had been chewing vigorously on his plug, and now in his excitement he spat vigorously at a loose clump of sage, but missed, splattering tobacco juice all over his own boot.

"Shit!"

"Watch it!" snapped Bart. "Or you'll be gettin' another busted-up lip." But he did not remove the glasses from his eyes.

Coke was thinking, "The sonofabitch's got eyes all over his head. Don't have to look to see somethin'." And he knew it to be true. Their leader was a man of astounding perception, especially at unexpected moments.

"They're pulling out," Bart said, his big jaw moving slowly over the words, which were mixed with his chew of—it seemed to him—a real prime cut of tobacco.

"What's that feller doin'?" Coke asked.

"Standing there."

"What's he doin', fer Chrissakes?" demanded Coke, aware that he was pushing, yet somehow not minding it. He'd been feeling feisty a good while now, and he knew Gooden could feel it. Well, tough.

"He's standing there scratching his ass, you stupid bastard." Bart Gooden lowered the glasses slowly, his eyes still on the ranch house and the man below.

Slowly he swung his big head around to look at Coke Millers. "Want to get yer clock cleaned, do you?"

"I ain't afraid of you, Bart. I do my work, and I ain't afraid of you."

Remembering the action later, Harelip couldn't recollect seeing Bart Gooden get to his feet, but suddenly the big man was up and had brought his fist up from the ground. He slammed Coke somewhere, the guts maybe, and the man doubled with a terrible grunt, all the wind knocked out of him. Then Bart had brought up his knee, right into Coke's bent over face, and another fist pole-axed Coke Millers right there in his tracks. By golly, Harelip told it all later, that man Coke dropped like a dead man. His face red, pulpy, and bleeding especially after the boot his leader instantly drove into him while he was lying on the ground.

Bart stood looking down at the prone Coke Millers. "Bugger shouldn't talk back to his ramrod. You mind that, Harelip. You tell the others. Any you men don't like the job, then get yer ass on the trail—like right now!"

"Got'cha." Harelip got the word out almost before Bart had finished speaking. There was, mind you, no sense to argue with that man, 'specially when he had a burr up his ass.

They were silent a moment, looking down at the fallen Coke Millers.

"What you want done with him?" Harelip asked.

"Pack him back to the outfit. He ain't quit workin' for Prairie Dog."

"Good enough." Harelip spat, nodded, adjusted his hat, and scratched swiftly at his crotch.

"First we'll see what that feller down there's up to."

"The boys delivered the message," Harelip said, clearly puzzled. "Don't 'pear to me that feller can do anything about anything."

"Mebbe." Bart Gooden was again looking through the glasses. "But he suspicions somethin'."

Harelip tried to purse his lips in surprise, but because of his infirmity was not able. This did not lessen his astonishment at the other man's insight into what was going on in that man's mind down there at the DV Range.

"What you figger?"

Gooden lowered the field glasses. "That feller is suspicioning somethin'."

"How the hell kin you tell that?"

"Tell by the way he's standin' there. He ain't satisfied. He figgers somethin's up." He lifted the glasses and looked down at the lone figure standing outside the cabin. The man was looking at the Appaloosa pony in the corral.

"That's it," Bart said.

"What?"

"The damn hoss told him," Bart Gooden said, muttering the words in disgust. "Shit!"

But Harelip Thoms, no dumbbell, also heard the streak of—what?—maybe envy, in Bart Gooden's voice.

Bart lowered his glasses. "Shit take it."

"Which way," Harelip said after a long moment of silence.

But Gooden didn't answer. He was looking through the glasses again.

A long moment passed.

"He'll wait till dark," Gooden said.

"Whyn't we ride down and take him?" Harelip asked. His eyes were on Coke Millers who was coming around.

But his boss was shaking his head. He lifted the glasses again and bent all his attention to the scene below them.

After another long moment Bart said, "You and Coke there, you ride back to the outfit. Whistle up some help. Maybe get Hen Bowles and them."

"Them that was down there already?"

Bart Gooden disdained a verbal reply and simply belched as he lowered the glasses. "I'll be here, keepin' a eye on it meanstwhile."

"You smellin' trouble, are you?" Harelip asked, speaking carefully, as was his way with Bart Gooden.

His leader did not deign to answer the direct question. Instead, he lowered the glasses and slipped them back in the case that was on the ground beside him.

Another moment passed while Harelip listened to his companion sucking his teeth; obviously as an aid to thought.

"Ever hear the name Slocum?" Gooden asked, reaching for his makings.

"No."

"John Slocum."

"Can't say I know the name."

"Feller s'posed to 've rode with Nate Champion during the cattle war."

Harelip's puckered brow cleared. "Now that you mention it . . ." He jerked his head suddenly. "That him? Down there? You know him?"

Bart Gooden was silent, building his smoke slowly between his calloused fingers. Then, with one stroke he twisted the end of the cigarette, licked it along its length, and let it hang from the corner of his mouth. Harelip admired how not a one of those thick black nails got in the way.

Reaching up, Gooden took a wooden lucifer out of his hatband and struck it one-handed across his thumbnail.

"I'd say ten'd get you twenty on it," Bart said. "Plus that man 'pears to favor a sorrel as I recollect. Dodge it was. Not too long back." He had taken the glasses out of their case again.

This gesture was not lost on his companion, who remarked silently that, whoever it was down there, his boss Bart Gooden had suddenly caught a burr under his saddle.

"You git goin'," Gooden said. "I'll keep a eye on him."

Slocum, turning quickly on his heel in answer to that extra sense that sometimes touched him, caught the twinkle of sunlight on the ledge where the steep slope leading up from the DV Range ended, just from the corner of his eye. He did not turn to verify it, but remained as he was, looking at the Appaloosa. Then, checking the position of the sun, he figured how much time until dark. A good hour. He knew he was only just in rifle shot, but just. A careful bushwhacker could maybe risk it, especially if he had a Sharps.

He paused, looked casually around as though checking on possible chores, then, careful not to move in a straight line for a leading shot, he walked around the cabin to have a look-see. Calling out to the women to let him in, he entered the kitchen.

"What's up?" Dolly's gimlet eyes were right on him, suspicious, demanding.

"Somebody up on that ledge by the timberline with glasses," he said. His eyes were on the girl, noting how she was even more attractive than before.

"Them fellers took off in a hurry," Dolly observed. "What did you tell them?"

"Told them to git."

Sally was already pouring coffee into the three mugs that they'd left on the table when the visitors had arrived.

"They'll be back," Dolly Dolores said, and she sniffed loudly. "The pigs! They surely stink up a place."

Sally spoke as she seated herself at the kitchen table. "Why don't you stay a while? You can use that cabin Dolly told you, the bunkhouse. And there's game for supper."

"Good enough."

She took a drink of coffee and put down her mug. "I've got a few chores to tend to."

"Don't go outside," Slocum said, lifting a hand as though to stop any movement on her part.

"Why not?" She had half risen from her chair and now sat back.

"You seen somethin' out there," Dolly said. "But

why can't she? There's something else, ain't there? Not just that one up by the timber."

"I took a look at the tracks those horses made, and there were seven who rode in, but only six rode out."

"That why they were so many?" Dolly asked. "To cover it?"

"That's what I figure. He's in the barn. The Appaloosa gave him away."

"You go near there an' he can shoot you easy as a sitting jay," Dolly said.

"That's what I know."

"So what can one man do?" she asked. "That six or seven couldn't?"

Slocum took a pull at his coffee. "He can bushwhack any one of us. Only he won't do that."

"Why not?" Dolly Dolores snapped out the words as though she was biting them.

"On account of he could have done it already and didn't. Even so, we don't want to give him a chance. He could change his mind. Also, he can draw our attention to himself instead of the barn."

"So what are they planning then?" She stood up. "I'm setting right here by the window and keeping a bead on that sonofabitch. If he takes one step outside, I am blasting him to hell!"

"I'd make a guess he's figuring to fire the place." Slocum said it as though he was just telling the time of day, and then sat back watching the effect of his words on his two hostesses.

"Fire the place!" Dolly was staring at him in astonishment. "What the hell for!"

"That's easy. To get you out of here."

She stared at him in tight silence. And even

though he wasn't looking at Sally, he could feel the girl's eyes on him.

"Jesus . . ." The word broke softly from Dolly Dolores's loose lips. "Jesus . . ."

"And the man up on the ridge?" Sally asked. And he saw her face tighten, especially around her eyes, which seemed larger, more brown. God, she was good looking!

"He's covering," Dolly said before Slocum could speak.

But the girl was looking at him, paying no mind to her sister.

"That's it," Slocum said. "And he could be packing a Sharps for the range."

He stood up, reaching into his pocket for a lucifer. "Just act ordinary," he said. "Like now, it's evening, and you'll be fixing supper, and we'll eat it and go to bed. Like that. Just like everything's the way it usually is."

"But what about the girls?" Dolly asked suddenly. "Emily and Ruth, and that other . . ." She bent her head, trying to remember the name. "Fay. Yeah. What about them?"

"Let them be. If they know about this they're likely to act funny, and then our visitor will get suspicious."

"But . . ."

"Let me handle it," Slocum said swiftly. "Now just act natural and stay away from the window. Dunno if you're hungry, but we'll act like we're having supper and turning in. See?"

"And then?" Dolly's tone was tight as wire.

"I'll handle it."

"But the girls?" Sally said. "I . . . I don't know

them, but if there's something I can do . . ."

"Sal's only been here a couple weeks," Dolly said. "She don't know her way around yet."

But her sister wasn't listening to her. She was looking at Slocum, waiting for instructions. "I can go be with them if it's any help," she said.

He smiled at her, glad to see her courage and quiet good sense. While her sister had started to pace the floor cussing and arguing the situation out loud.

"I told those fools Gooden would pull some kind of game. They wouldn't listen. Torgerson and Cole and Flint too. Told 'em! Warned the idiots how Bart Gooden was up to no good snooping around like he was, pretending he was interested in homesteading, building a spread, settling in the country. Like that. Shit! I spotted that bugger right now. Saw through him. I mean, right now! Knew he was up to no good! Fact, he come by one night to visit the girls and tried to get out without paying. I was ready to shoot the damn crook. But he finally come across!" She ran her tongue across her dry lips, sniffed, nodded her head a couple of times, and took her hat off.

Slocum didn't think she looked all that different with it off. Her hair was still wild, and anyway it was actually her eyes that took over her face. They were like bronze beads. Yet, at the same time, he detected a certain softness around her mouth. He held his surprise in check; Dolly Dolores VanDam was nobody to get previous with. And he almost grinned at her as he found her sharp eyes trying to read him.

"I'll go over and check the girls," Dolly said moving swiftly to the door. "You stay here. Slocum, she's a greenhorn, but she got good blood in her."

When the door had closed behind Dolly, Slocum said, "Your sister acts tough, but you likely know more than me that she likes you."

"I do know." She smiled quietly at him. "You know, we're not real sisters, but I believe we get along better than if we were."

"Yes, I felt that," Slocum said.

"I was adopted by Dolly's parents. A good while back now, it seems." And the smile at the corners of her mouth gave him the urge to walk over and kiss her. But he checked himself.

"Doll left home a good while ago, when I was still small. Then we didn't hear from her. We didn't know where she was. When our parents died, I decided to find her."

"I can see you're glad you did. Am I right?"

"Yes, I'm glad. But I must say, it was kind of a surprise. I had no idea she was . . . well . . . doing what she's doing. I guess . . . it's all right . . ." She looked down at her hands. And he could see the wistful smile just at the corner of her mouth.

But it was no time for romance as he stepped quickly to the side of the window so that he could see the barn.

"You've got stock?" he asked.

"The horses and a team and then a few head of cattle. Dolly, well you see, Dolly took cattle sometimes and even a horse in payment for . . ." Her voice broke off.

"I see." He had turned back from the window. "Do you think maybe there's more to Gooden's pushing than just that he wants your sister's land?"

"You mean?" She looked at him in surprise, evidently not having thought that deeply into the reasons for Bart Gooden's aggressive behavior.

"Maybe something to do with her business?" He nodded in the direction of the rear cabin.

"I never thought of that. You see, I don't know anything really about Dolly's business, except . . . well, what you see." And she looked away from his direct gaze, her cheeks coloring.

"Listen, it's a way to make a living. I don't recommend it. But it's a hard world for some people, and that's what's there. You can't always find so-called respectable women who are as honest or straight as some of the what they call soiled doves."

"I'm sure. I'm sure of that. I didn't mean . . ."

But the door opened then, and Dolly came in. "I've warned the girls. Told 'em they could come over here and join us, but told 'em to wait till I talked with you. We sure don't want to excite that sonofabitch in the barn." And she glared at the two of them from under her thick, battle-ready eyebrows. "Though I'd be happy to shoot a load of blue whistlers into his goddamn ass!" And she glared around the room as though looking for a place to spit her disgust.

"Are there more men out there, do you think?" Sally asked, turning to Slocum.

"Well, there's the one who's been watching us with his field glasses. But others? Maybe those that rode in here, but I doubt it. They'll want to fire the place, run off what stock you have, but they don't appear to want to make an open attack. Otherwise they'd run the risk of raising a storm all through the valley. This way, if it's a fire, it could be blamed on some of Tall Bear's young bucks on the prod. I wouldn't be surprised if there'd be some sign stashed around, an arrow or two. Like that." He turned toward Dolly Dolores. "You got any notion how come they want to get you out of here?"

"I told you. I mean, if you got ears to hear it. Land. Range. And water too. And don't you fergit it. I got the best way to the water right through that northern strip we rode cross when we come down."

"Then why don't they just do it openly?"

"No guts, that's why."

But Slocum wasn't satisfied. "Have they been complaining about your business out here?"

"If they have I sure haven't heard it. And judging by the customers that stop by, it don't look like complaint to me. I ain't getting rich, but we ain't starvin' neither."

Slocum studied it. There was something missing. Sure, the riders and hands around the outfits would want to patronize Dolly's establishment, and there would be those who would ride out from Hardtown, it wasn't that much of a distance anyway. But there was some other reason why somebody didn't want her business there. And he wasn't at all sure that the vinegary old dame didn't know who, what, and why. But she wasn't letting any of it on. For sure, too, she wasn't going to give an inch. Slocum admired it, but he had no intention of letting that sour, crusty individual under that extraordinary hat get even a whiff of what he was thinking.

"Time to light a lamp," he said.

3

Royal Thor Undershaft held the paper well above the red-hot stove. At the same time he was fully aware of the strong vapors from the burning coffee beans that were filling the room. With mounting excitement he watched the surface of the paper gradually take on a faint yellowish tint.

His heart bounded. This was it! This was precisely what he had been striving for. It was the coffee beans that had pulled the trick. It was just that yellow tint that made the paper look old. Plus it made the writing on the paper look sufficiently aged for his purpose.

For months the scheme had been forming in his mind. It would bring everything he needed, everything he wanted. The word *power* slipped into his mind, and he smiled. Why, with that kind of wealth he could pick and choose exactly what he wished, and even more important, who.

He put down the yellowed paper, took a slim cigar, a panatela, out of his coat pocket and bit off the little bullet at the end. Holding it for a moment on the end of his tongue, he spat it neatly into the shiny brass spittoon near his feet. Looking down now at the spittoon, then at his polished Wellington boots, he experienced a little bounce of joy as he thought of how well his plan was working. And with his middle finger, he reached up and wiped his bottom lip where a fleck of saliva had found a place. Yes, neat. His thumb and forefinger touched the crisp, brush mustache that covered completely the ugly scar on his upper lip. The dark brown bristles did more. They covered a past that more than just a handful of people would have given a great deal to unearth.

Crossing the room now he stood looking at himself in the large oval mirror that hung on the wall behind the horsehair sofa, regarding himself through the surge of self-satisfaction that had taken over completely. He enjoyed the view, pleased that the high heels he'd specially ordered gave him the height that he required, especially now as his coup began to bear fruit. A man of fifty, he thought, but looking a good bit younger. Ten years maybe. Well, surely five! Yes, a mature forty-five. The slightly sloped forehead added a dividend of dignity, supporting the stern walk, the deep, plangent voice, and upon occasion, the malacca cane carried under his arm, according to mood.

Suddenly remembering, he stepped quickly back to the stove and picked up the paper and studied it. It needed more. Not quite good enough. His requirements were exacting. Shortly, when the paper showed the precise tint, he swept the coffee beans from the stove and filled the kitchen sink with water. He submerged the paper for its next step, a good soak.

While that part of the operation was in progress he prepared for the aging process that he had worked out through his many experiments. He placed a thin sheet of asbestos on the stove. When the yellowed paper was thoroughly soaked, he laid it on the asbestos, then placed a second sheet of asbestos over it and weighted it with stones. Humming to himself now, he filled a small cloth bag with fine soil dust that he had ground up in a mortar. He stood back. All he had to do now was wait for the paper to dry completely, and he could complete the last stage of its treatment.

Royal Thor Undershaft, born Jake Hinds, had not the slightest concern over how his scheme might wreak havoc on those he dispossessed of their lawful property. That was their concern. His was the matter of his own profit plus the fine image he would now polish and present to an admiring public. Royal Thor Undershaft! Not a name that could be found in the common run of names. Indeed, it had taken a lot of work to find it. But somehow, seeing it in a catalogue from a company selling advantage tools for the gambling fraternity, the name took over. It was unique, mysterious, and since Undershaft happened to be the name of a company, long defunct, that had manufactured loaded dice, and Thor happened to be the god of thunder and war he had found in both the image he wished to create. The addition of "Royal" spoke for itself.

He had, of course, wanted a name that would be totally unique, a name that no one else anywhere,

ever, could have claimed. And he was always well
aware how the sound of that powerful monicker
arrested people's attention, gave them pause to
realize that by God they were not dealing with
just anybody.

And to be sure, such a handle required money
to support it! He grinned, admiring his height in
the mirror as at the same time he felt the actuality
of the lifts in his boots. His grin widened as he
thought of those sheets of asbestos on the hot stove,
between which was the paper that would make him
wealthy, feared, and above all, respected!

It had taken just about ten minutes from the
time he had set the forged paper to dry, and now it
was ready. He shook the cloth bag above it, sifting
dust onto the paper, then rubbed the dirt in with
a rag.

The finished result was all that he could have
hoped for. The document was one of the most
impressive he'd ever seen. It was equal to, even
better than some of the land grants and other
treaty documents he'd studied in Cheyenne and
Chicago.

He stepped back now, his hands on his hips, surveying his work with pride. By damn! It was all
right! Again he walked to the mirror and regarded
the stocky figure, envisioning himself presenting
the land grant—though only if necessary. There
was always the chance that it might not be needed.
Indeed, he had a feeling that he could carry the
day without it. But, even so, it was there, added
ammunition. With it, he was absolutely assured of
the land he required, to which he alone had title,
plus the considerable surrounding area. An area

where cattle grazed, where ranches covered the rich prairie. The Half Circle Dot, the Double-Back K, the DV Range with that worthless, loudmouthed female who was getting away with murder running her sporting house right out in broad daylight on the prairie!

Torgerson, Cole, and Flint were another matter however. They were tough, but he knew he could do business with them—or could at least consider certain rules of the game. But with that old bitch, it wasn't that easy. She was trouble, mostly because she understood nothing of the rules of the game. With a man like Torgerson, for instance, well he was a sonofabitch, no question, but he used the standard weapons like any man would.

To be sure, they wanted too much money. But he knew they'd come around. They'd have to. Besides, he had his documents. Flint was the easiest; Torgerson and Cole were tough, but he'd simply apply the pressure. The thing was, he'd put the pressure on VanDam first to give them a taste of what was in store. That old bitch of a crow!

Suddenly he felt an itch in his crotch, and as he reached down to scratch with one hand, with the other he took out his horologe from his vest pocket and looked at the time. It was just then there came the expected knock at the door. Right on time!

Royal Thor Undershaft was all smiles as his hand reached the knob and turned it.

"You're late," he said, with a big grin widening his narrow face.

Her eyes dropped down to his waist. "I'm sorry, Bunny," as she reached down and squeezed the bulge in his trousers. "I wouldn't dream of keeping him waiting . . ."

It was unbelievable! Incredible! And Royal Thor Undershaft was definitely a man who not only understood the meaning of those words, but also used them in conversation as well as in thought. Incredible that in only the span of a flashing instant he had totally lost any contact whatsoever with the great thoughts that had been gripping him as he'd surveyed himself in the mirror on the wall in his office at the Frontier Cottage in Hardtown. All that self-praise, all those plans for the future, imagined pictures of how his life was now going to be, all had simply vanished.

In its place, the raging cyclone of his passion had totally claimed him as he stood totally naked behind his erection while his completely naked companion on her knees before him mounted him with her mouth.

Royal could hardly stand. His shaking legs, spread wide as he received her plunging lips, mouth, tongue and throat, kept him afoot only by the slimmest margin. His moans of exquisite joy mixed with her wet, sucking noises, as she almost choked on her delirious pleasure, yet executed her part of the exquisite dance with such superb artistry that her fluttering tongue never missed a beat.

Then all at once and in perfect unison they collapsed together in their consummate timing, exploding as the tornado of passion fluid drenched them.

How long the silence lasted neither knew as they lay, still entwined, their bodies shiny with perspiration and come while they regained their breath.

"Oh, my God," she murmured. "Did you lock the door?"

"Of course not!"

Her laughter tinkled against his ear. "You are a devil, Roy. A devil!"

She raised up on an elbow and looked down into his face, her long blonde hair falling into his eyes, and at the same time one firm, rosy nipple found his lips. He began to suck.

"Oh my God, if you do that we'll never get that door locked. Oh!"

"That's what I know," he said, speaking with her nipple and some of the rest of her delicious teat in his mouth.

"I want you inside me this time."

"But of course."

They had shifted positions again so that now she was on top with her legs spread so that she was astride his hard body. His erection was riding right along the crack between her buttocks, which were soaked with come. But in an instant she had mounted him, riding down on his great shaft, and then up and down again, and up and down and upanddownandupanddownandandand . . .

"The door is still not locked," she whispered into his ear as they both sank into oblivion.

They were fast asleep in each other's arms and legs when the door opened quietly and a head looked in. It was a man's head, and the expression of caution on the face turned instantly to astonishment, and then glee. He was a ruddy-faced man with thick, wiry eyebrows. He came all the way into the room, closing the door carefully behind him. He took pains to make no sound that would attract either the naked pair on the floor or anyone passing in the corridor outside the room; all his attention was on the silence with which he closed the door. He could hear only his own breathing.

When he turned away from the door again he found himself staring into the round barrel of the Smith & Wesson his employer was holding casually in his hand.

"Charles! Will you never learn? That was stupid of you!"

Luckily, the moon wasn't yet up, though Slocum could see his way. It had taken him a while to reach the far side of the barn. The Appaloosa was still standing in the round horse corral, though now and again looking toward the door of the barn, but making no move to enter. Slocum hoped the horse wouldn't nicker as he approached. That was the trouble with getting him onto oats—it always turned out he'd want some and would let you know, with that deep-throated nicker. Suddenly, and for no reason at all as far as he could tell, he remembered Buck, the feisty buckskin cowpony, who was so tough he refused oats. Buck was one of the first mustangs Slocum had broken, and he'd done a good job. But he could never get Buck to go for the rattling can of oats with which he'd try to attract him so he could throw a halter on him.

He moved slowly, silent as his own breath, silent enough to feel the land breathing, hunched over, moving quickly from one cover to another—the watering trough, the pile of manure, the stack of building logs. Not much for cover, but he was lucky; or, he decided, the man in the barn just wasn't very sharp.

And it just took him a while. He was also counting on the chance that the man in the barn was figuring the trick of riding in with a bunch of horsemen had fooled them, that neither himself nor the two women had any suspicion of someone extra having come along. It was a good enough trick, but old. And as far as a man like John Slocum was concerned, any trick that had worked once was so old that it shouldn't be tried again. For sure, the seven who had ridden in hadn't any way of knowing that he was onto such niceties. In other words, it spelled out to him that they weren't all that bright, though they were dangerous nonetheless. In fact, it was the dumb members of the outlaw gentry who were the most dangerous. As a rule, you could tell what a man with some good horse sense was going to do; with the other kind you couldn't.

He was close enough to the barn now that he could hear a pack rat scampering after something or other, likely oats, or maybe some old harness, or for the matter of that, it could be money. He'd known a pack rat to steal silver dollars from a saddlebag he'd left in a livery. He was also thinking how that pack rat could be a help to him as a cover for any untoward sound that might raise the suspicion of his quarry.

He was right up against the side of the barn now, with one hand feeling the rough, unpeeled logs. He could hear the man inside: a stifled sneeze, a striking match. The fool. Tobacco could be smelled

from a distance. It told him something of the low
caliber of the man. He wondered whether the man
had his horse with him inside the barn.

He had the feeling of the man being a bit nervous,
impatient, and maybe even resentful that he'd been
chosen for the particular job. Slocum had assumed
the job would be the firing of the barn and possibly
more, although he was pretty sure they wouldn't try
to fire the other buildings. The action was supposed
to be a threat, at least as far as he could figure it.

It occurred to him, stretching it to be sure, that
there could maybe be more than one man in the
barn. It would mean that two men had ridden in
on one horse.

He had been stealing along the side of the barn
and was now next to the big, open doorway, a
great black hole in the moonless night. He waited,
listening. Hearing only his own breath and, now
again from inside the barn, the scratch of a match.
This time he caught the flare through a crack
between the logs where the chinking had fallen
out—the outline of the man's head and cupped
hand as he bent to the settling flame. Then he
caught the odor of coal oil. So the barn was to
be fired. He supposed now that the man's horse
would be staked a good distance away from the
barn. That would have made sense. Though it was
possible that the horse might be inside the barn
and that its owner would lead it out before going
about his grisly job. But the man was making no
sound that indicated he was about to lead a horse
outside, nor did Slocum catch any indication of
a horse in there with him. No, Slocum decided, the
horse was picketed outside, and the man was alone

in the barn, along with the pack rat.

And then? Would the gang return to make sure the job was going well? Likely not, for they would then risk leaving evidence that would show they'd been there—telltale prints around the barn which could be traced to the owners' horses. More likely, the man would set the fire and make his escape, probably with his companions covering him from a distance. Like the man he'd spotted on the ledge watching through the glasses. Besides, pursuit wouldn't be possible unless Dolly and her sister were going to try to catch the fire-setter rather than stay and fight the fire.

Clearly, there was only one way to handle the situation. It certainly wasn't one he favored, but there was no alternative. Anyhow there was no time to waste. The man in the barn was already spreading the coal oil.

Half-crouching now, Slocum moved swiftly across the space that lay between himself and the barn, while the man inside was making his final preparations before torching the building.

He moved as quickly as he could, yet wary of anything that might be in the way as he worked around to the open doorway.

Now he heard a movement inside. A horse? No, it had to be the man. He smelled the coal oil more strongly. His hunch had been right.

"That you, Kelly?"

Those three words saved Slocum's life, for they verified what he had been already suspecting—that there was a second man, outside the barn, somewhere in the corral more than likely, who was playing backup for the fireman inside.

Even as he just caught those words, Slocum felt the movement behind him, and the whistle of air as the barrel of the gun just missed his head. His sixth sense had again saved him by a fraction of an inch.

Spinning, he saw the figure lunging at him, and without an instant's hesitation, he brought his boot up and kicked. A sound, half grunt, half squeal, and all pain, broke from the man who had tried to lay him out with the shooting iron.

"Kelly!"

The voice was sharper, edged with alarm. Suddenly the dark figure filled the doorway.

"That you, Kelly?" But there was no power in the hurried question, as though the man already knew the answer.

He had no time for reaction. Slocum stepped quickly alongside him and jammed the barrel of his .44 in his ribs. The man let out a gasp of pain.

Slocum quickly disarmed him.

"Anyone else out there?" And he jammed the barrel of the Colt deeper into the man's ribs.

"No. No, there ain't." The voice was shaking, yet surly.

"Sure!"

"Mister, there ain't nobody out there, 'less you brought him with you."

"If there is," snapped Slocum, "you're a dead man."

"Mister . . . there ain't nobody." The voice had become a whine.

With the barrel of the Colt, Slocum pushed his captive in the direction of the fallen Kelly, who was only now beginning to moan and come round.

"On your feet. And both of you walk right in front of me, but side by side. You hear me!"

They heard. There was no hesitating at all; they did it exactly as he told it.

"If there is anyone out there—now you hear me!— I will take you both apart, and you'll never get back together again. You understand me!"

"Yup . . ."

"You!" Slocum jammed the gun barrel into the second man.

"I . . . do . . ." And he began to cough.

With their backs to him, he searched swiftly for any more weaponry as they halted in front of the cabin door.

"It's me," he called out. "Slocum. Open up. I've got a couple of visitors." He added quickly, "But stand away from the doorway. There's still that one up on the ledge, and he could have a Sharps, so douse your light before opening."

"Shit," said one of his prisoners. "Shit, Slocum. You're too damn smart! There ain't anybody up there."

"How do you know there isn't?" Slocum snapped back.

"On account of Bart said . . ."

"Shut yer mouth!" suddenly hissed his companion. "Fer Chrissakes, Tobin, what the hell you doin' runnin' off yer mouth!"

"Go fuck yerself."

"And you watch your mouth, mister," warned Slocum as the door opened. And he was gratified to see that the women had followed his instructions and that there was no light showing.

"Inside!" He jabbed the gun barrel into the nearest man's ribs, receiving in return a grunt of pain and a curse.

Only when the door was closed and bolted did Slocum ask the women to light one of the coal oil lamps. As soon as the flame brought the kitchen into view, he said, "Maybe you'd both better go into the other room. I want to question these two."

"Sally . . ." Dolly Dolores turned her head swiftly and glared at her sister. "You got that sewin' to tend to."

"And you too," Slocum said.

"Mister, this is my house. And this here is my outfit. I am settin' right here to listen to what these two scum have got to tell about who sent them!"

Slocum had been watching the girl, admiring her restraint, realizing that though she was obviously fearful of what was unfolding, she was not terrified. His eyes were on her as she left the kitchen without a word.

Slocum turned to his hostess then. "Can you handle that goose gun?" His eyes dropped to the shotgun that was leaning against the edge of the kitchen table where Dolly had stood it.

"That's a dumb question," she retorted hotly.

"Then you can stay."

"Thanks!" The word was rigid with sarcasm as she glared at the man who had taken over and was giving orders.

"You keep these two covered while I take a look-see that there's nobody else hanging around."

"That's a good idea, mister." The words were still loaded.

"I'll be back directly," he said. And added, as he started to the door, "Just in case they might take a notion to up and start something." And he looked at her hand resting on the barrel of the shotgun.

"They won't start anything," Dolly Dolores said. "Not with this load of blue whistlers lookin' at them."

4

Some folks allowed that Hardtown was a boomtown. But then that was said about a lot of places in Wyoming if there happened to be a house or two. But Hardtown had thirty or maybe a couple more houses, some of sod, some of packing boxes, and some of real lumber. It was built where the old Stinking Water Trading Post used to be, only a few miles from Fort Harrison.

The main building in town was The Best Time Saloon. Next to it stood Saul Kincaid's blacksmith shop. Down the street a piece, with nothing but the weather in between was Amos Hohnlicker's general store, and across the rutted street from Hohnlicker's squatted the Smith Hotel. At the far end there were three more saloons, but Slocum saw right off that the place of action was The Best Time. For not only was it the largest drinking establishment, but it was obviously the center where he knew he could pick up on the local gossip and rumors and get the feel of the town and the surrounding countryside.

This notion was borne out as he passed through the batwing doors and found himself in a veritable logjam of humanity. Everyone seemed to be talking at once, and it took him a moment to discover that he was attending a trial for murder and that the action was going to begin at any moment.

The facts, as much as he could glean, were these. Recently, a man named McGee had been shot to death on the premises by a man named Mulvaney over an altercation at cards. McGee, it was avowed, had been armed with five aces; Mulvaney with a Smith & Wesson. The Smith & Wesson had taken the hand. But the trial had been delayed for some while until the defendant had been able to acquire a lawyer, who had come to Hardtown all the way from Cheyenne.

The astonishing factor was that while a good dozen witnesses had actually seen Mulvaney whip out a pistol and shoot the unarmed McGee, killing him instantly, Mulvaney's attorney had entered a plea of Not Guilty. This had brought the room to the uproar into which Slocum had arrived.

Mulvaney's attorney, a tall, willowy man with a great white mane of hair and a name to match it—Elihu Lincoln Thong—stood with dignity at the center of the big room with the crowd pressing in on him. Several times, the sheriff had to order people back so that there would be room for the trial to proceed.

Thong was an impressive man. Dressed in a long, heavy black overcoat that came all the way down to the floor, he wore a muffler around his neck and spectacles almost at the end of his nose. His costume caused some comment among the crowd, for the day was hot, and it seemed rather strange for the defense attorney to be dressed as though it were January rather than June.

It was the final day of the trial. The prosecutor had just finished his summation, and it was now the moment for the defense to speak.

Summoned by the judge to step forward, Thong rose, tall as a tree it seemed to Slocum, with his shiny head bobbing on top of the long, black overcoat. He had heard that Thong had proclaimed his client's innocence from the start, maintaining that the dead man, McGee, had not been killed by the bullet from Mulvaney's gun, but had died on the spot from a heart attack, before the bullet struck him.

Now Thong reiterated his claim, going over it point by point, to the murmuring of the crowd who made no effort to disguise their astonishment at neither the appearance nor the argument of the strange man from Cheyenne.

Having again stated his brief, the defending counsel whipped off his overcoat with a great flourish and stood in the middle of the makeshift courtroom naked to the waist. He offered an astonishing sight to the bug-eyed spectators. His upper torso was painted in an extraordinary variety of brilliant colors outlining the major internal organs of the body—the heart, the lungs, the liver, the stomach, and the kidneys.

Using the colored artwork on his body as graphic illustration, Thong described at great length the purposes and functions of each organ and its relationship to the others. His absolutely sure manner

and professional-sounding pronounciation of the
difficult technical terms held the jury in thrall.
His description of how fear had gripped McGee
and had paralyzed his functioning, thus causing
death, was masterful. For almost an hour he held
them spellbound and convinced them that he was
indeed a superior medical authority, the like of
which none of them had ever encountered.

Slocum could not detect a single person unaf-
fected by Thong's astounding onslaught and realized that it was a performance he would not soon
forget.

It led inevitably to Thong's final deposition: that
the deceased had not died as a result of the defendant's "intemperate bullet"; he had died of a heart
attack before the bullet struck him, even before he
hit the floor. Rising in a crescendo, the defender's
blood-and-thunder voice came to a crashing climax,
bringing the listeners figuratively to their knees
and the entire room to an awesome silence.

Not a sound. No one knew where to look, much
less what to say. Suddenly, someone released an
extravagant giggle, but it swiftly disappeared back
into the awesome silence.

The redoubtable Thong rose once more from his
chair. Pointing his long arm and bony finger dra-
matically at the defendant, his agate-colored eyes
flashed as he addressed the mute gathering, "Reject
not the command of the Lord! Judge not, that ye be
not judged!"

This last onslaught was too much; court was
adjourned until the following morning.

Slocum closed in on the bar, bought himself a
whiskey, and moved down to one end where he had

a good view of the room. He decided that Hardtown was a place he could take. It was definitely a town with a sense of humor. He grinned as he stood leaning against the bar listening to the thrum of the wheel of fortune, the calling of the faro dealer, the clink of chips, the thump of the ivories hitting the green baize on the dice table, each sound in its own way redefining the event that had just taken place.

Elihu Lincoln Thong, covered in his enormous black overcoat, made his way through the crowd. The crowd applauded. Slocum, for his part, was delighted to see that the spindly, yet wholly vigorous lawyer gave this recognition not the slightest notice.

The great thing about a good saloon, Slocum had often observed, was that the basic line that all shared was reconciliation. Clearly, the typical saloon bore witness to the entire span of human behavior: good and bad, saintly and devilish. All roads met here, all behavior was equalized. The saloon was the true melting pot, or as some evangelist had put it, all human behavior could be witnessed in this intrepid environment, for here God and the Devil were able to meet, and man found definition for himself, for better or worse.

He stood now at the bar, now and again leaning an elbow, a forearm, now and then regarding the action through the big mirror behind the row of bottles, then turning and leaning his back against the mahogany, surveying the whole room casually, without missing a thing. He liked it. He liked feeling his way in this manner, getting the taste of a place—and the lively scene of the trial had put him into a fine mood.

Slocum had always found such locales helpful to reflection, to the sorting out of difficulties, the solving of problems. He discovered this to be so in his present circumstance.

Back in the DV kitchen he had quizzed his two prisoners with Dolly Dolores looking on in malevolent silence. There wasn't much to be gotten from them, only that Jed Torgerson and Casper Flint had hired them to spy on the DV and fire the barn. So they claimed.

This information had come after some good while of interrogation, and it was Tobin who divulged it, albeit with great reluctance. Kelly, under Slocum's lash, had agreed that it was true. Nor had they been part of the bunch that rode in to deliver the message to Dolly Dolores. The pair had come in on one horse and left their second mount picketed a distance from the barn.

It was then that Dolly Dolores had spoken up. "They're lying," she said firmly, and taking out a cigar, lighted it slowly, her fish-like eyes, under lowered lids, regarding the two with loathing.

"You're working for Gooden," Slocum said. "I know that. And you know it. Now you get back to Gooden with a message. You tell him to keep away from the DV. You hearing me?"

They nodded. "Don't know Gooden, mister. But we hear you," the one named Kelly said.

And his companion said, "Who do we say?"

"Just tell him the man you met unexpectedly. The man who if he catches you anywhere near this range again will make you regret it. You hear that!" His eyes, his words, his whole body drove those words into the pair. And indeed one took a step backward, and the other shifted about on his feet.

"Pigs," Dolly Dolores said and blew out a cloud of cigar smoke.

"No, they're not pigs," Slocum said.

"What the hell are they then!" she demanded angrily, her face reddening.

"Pigs don't act that way," Slocum said. "You call them pigs, then what are you going to call the pigs?"

And he had sent them packing, to his hostess's delight. Presently, Dolly regaled her younger sister with the events with a good bit of vulgarity for extra measure.

He had been reluctant to ride off the next morning and made the women promise to keep on the alert. He'd even tried persuading Sally to come into town, to no avail.

"I want to stay with my sister," she'd insisted.

And as she'd said it he could tell how she'd also wanted to be with him. It hadn't made parting any easier.

"The thing is, I still don't see why they so badly want you out of here," he'd said to Dolly. "Why do they have to have the DV?"

"I told you, fer Chrissakes. Gooden and whoever it is backin' the sonofabitch want my girls. That's what the problem is. 'Course, they want the range too, more than likely. But I know for a fact he wants the girls. Hell, you know what a shortage there is of women in the Territory. About one for twenty-five. Hell, if a girl put out all night long she'd still have a line waiting for her from here to Texas in the morning."

"But he wants land too," Slocum had insisted.

"The others do, for a fact. Torgerson and Flint and Cole and all. Shit, they want it all!" And she opened the door and spat furiously.

"Dolly!"

It was a surprise to Slocum to see Sally McQuarie angry.

"Sorry. Forgot . . ." And Dolly Dolores turned to Slocum with a giant sigh, until all three had burst out laughing.

He had left reluctantly, planning to return as soon as he could. He had faith that Dolly Dolores was the equal of any two men—perhaps when fully enraged, even more. Now, right up close to the long mahogany bar, he spotted a little man with garters on the sleeves of his striped shirt coming toward him.

"You Slocum?"

"Who wants to know?" Slocum asked softly. He had been leaning back with his elbow on the bar while taking in the big room, which was still jammed with people. Though his eyes had been on the faro game off to his left, he'd picked up on the little man as soon as he appeared from a door at the back of the room.

"Mister Undershaft wants to see you," the man in pinstripes said.

"So . . ." And he remained leaning against the bar, while his right hand dropped a little toward his belt where he could reach the Colt in a short crossdraw.

"He's in the back room," the man said.

Slocum's eyes regarded him quietly and not with any obvious interest. He was thinking how quick they were, whoever they were.

For the first time, the pinstripe man looked baffled. His Adam's apple pumped in his long, thin throat.

"Mister Undershaft don't like to be . . ."

"Kept waiting," Slocum said, cutting in fast. "Tell Mister Undershaft that Mister Slocum says it's just as far from there to here as it is from here to there, see? And Mister Slocum doesn't like to be kept waiting either."

Suddenly, he felt something poke him in the back. It didn't feel like a gun barrel. When he turned, he found himself looking into the broad, heavy-boned face of the bartender, armed with a bungstarter.

"Mister . . ."

"I know. Mister Undershaft doesn't like to be kept waiting." And he shrugged and turned away.

But he had caught the look on one of the men who was standing nearby. Turning quickly he saw the bartender reaching again for the bungstarter, which he had put down on the bar.

In a trice, he vaulted up onto the bar and kicked the barman in the kidney. Then they were both down on the floor behind the bar, with Slocum pushing his knee against the other man's throat. The bartender was on his back gasping, his face russet with rage at having been caught.

"What say, mister?" Slocum asked. "Somebody wants to see me? Well tell him where I am!"

"That will be enough," a sharp voice suddenly said from the top of the bar, and raising up, Slocum saw the round hole in the barrel of the Colt Peace-maker looking down at him.

He got to his feet slowly, wiping his hands, keeping an eye on the prone barman who was still gasping for air.

"Come along," said the voice behind the gun. It was a crisp English voice, and the ruddy face under thick, wiry eyebrows was smiling coldly.

Slocum was up now. "No hard feelings, friend," he said looking down at the still gasping bartender, whose big belly was trying to pump air more quickly. "But I don't take kindly to such kinds of invites."

The fat bartender didn't answer.

Turning, Slocum looked at the bony man in the frock coat, who was still holding the Peacemaker. Beside him stood the man in the pinstripe shirt.

"By golly, your man seems mighty anxious to see me, don't he." Slocum had hoisted himself up onto the bar, swung his legs over, and dropped down on the other side. It was then he saw the tin star on the other man's coat.

"You're talkin' to the sheriff of Hardtown, Slocum. The name is Buck Charles. We'll be going to Mr. Undershaft's office where it will be quiet. Oh, and by the by, no guns in town. Except of course the law's."

"First I heard of it," Slocum said.

"It's the first the notice has been given," Charles said, as they both regarded the armaments amongst the gawking crowd.

"Well, I am not in the business of going against the law," Slocum said. "But first I want to see your papers. You look to be about as much a lawman as I'm a preacher."

The smile was thin-lipped, frosty, the pale blue eyes looked even bleaker. "Quite, sir." But he lowered the Peacemaker back into its holster inside the frock coat.

The expertise in the simple movement of returning the Colt to its holster was appreciated by Slocum. The importance of such details didn't escape him.

The voice sounded even more English as it said, "P'raps I had better take that gun of yours, sir, since it is the law."

A cold smile slipped into Slocum's eyes, then around his mouth. But he said nothing. Neither did he move.

"On the other hand," the sheriff of Hardtown pursued, "since Mister Undershaft is waiting, we'd better get along." He turned on his heel, offering a humorless smile to Slocum; while the crowd opened to allow passage as they crossed the room, Slocum noted something further about Undershaft's "sheriff": the man was slick as a whistle.

The room they entered was empty. Charles offered a seat carefully, his whole demeanor one of utmost seriousness.

It was an easychair that had been offered, but Slocum, careful not to let himself get comfortable, brought a straightback chair across the room and sat facing the desk and the big armchair behind it. He watched the flick of color enter the other man's cheeks as he did so. Good enough, he was thinking. It was always a good tactic to establish the ground oneself.

Charles crossed to the door behind the desk and, without opening it, knocked twice—obviously a sig-

nal—then came back and sat down in the chair
that Slocum had refused.

"You are a bull-headed man, Mister Slocum," he
said pleasantly. "I could've had my men overpower
you and take your gun, but since I didn't want to
build up an uproar in the room, I let it pass. But I
am telling you that while you're in Hardtown you'll
have to obey the law."

"And everyone in Hardtown will be giving up
their guns, will they?" Slocum's words cut across
to the man seated opposite him. "Come on, Sheriff."
He grinned wickedly at the man in the easychair.
"What happened to the real law in Hardtown? Or
was there ever any? Come on. Who's this man
Undershaft? Your boss, isn't he?" And his grin vanished. He sat back. "C'mon. Get him. I'm a busy
man."

Just at that moment the door situated behind the
desk opened, and a thin-faced man with a brush-like
mustache and deliberate walk entered the room.

"Mister Slocum? I am Royal Undershaft. No, sir,
don't get up!" He advanced, holding out a thin
hand, though Slocum hadn't made the slightest
move to get to his feet. Nor did he take the proffered hand.

And now, as Undershaft's hand dropped and a
tight smile touched his gaunt face, Slocum leaned
forward with his elbows on his knees, his eyes hard
on his host who seated himself carefully behind
his desk.

"Well, Undershaft, what is it you want?"

The lean man turned to Charles. "I think that will
be all, Sheriff." Swiftly turning to Slocum, he said, "I
do apologize, Mister Slocum, for any inconvenience

you've suffered. But from my point of view, it was necessary to get hold of you as quickly as possible before other, uh, parties took the initiative." He paused, waiting for Charles to leave. As the door closed, he returned his attention to Slocum.

"I really do apologize, you know. I'm new out here on the frontier, and of course it's going to take me a while to get the hang of things. Charles has smoothed the way somewhat, but of course being English—or at any rate, claiming he is—he hasn't been a great help." He shifted slightly in his chair. "I am suggesting that we start over, Slocum. Eh? How say?" Bending down, he opened a little closet at the bottom of his desk and brought out a decanter almost three-quarters filled with brown liquid.

"I know you're very taken up with the DV Range up on Miner Creek, and you very likely know some of the problems of its, uh, shall we say, salty owner . . . and I don't want to take up your time unduly. But I did want very much to talk to you, to make your acquaintance, and at the same time to introduce myself to you."

Slocum picked up instantly on the sudden hard ring that came into the voice. He said nothing. He had a good notion of what was coming, and he simply held his peace.

"I've heard a good bit about you, Slocum. And your name has always reached my attention with high recommendations."

Slocum continued his silence, suddenly feeling there had to be some connection between Undershaft and his strange adventure with the Rabbit Rock posse. He had an uneasy sense that his life was being spied on. Feeling something tighten inside him, he cautioned himself. It was not the time to react, but to stay free.

Undershaft had the decanter on the desk before him, with one hand loosely on it, but he made no move to lift the glass stopper.

He cleared his throat. "Briefly, I want to hire you. I need a man like you, of your caliber, and I am offering you a good-paying job. A job I consider extremely important that requires a man of your obvious talents and ability." He lifted the stopper now and began pouring the brown fluid into two glasses. "It's an excellent brandy, Slocum. I know you'll like it. Fact, I might be able to dig you up a bottle." And he sighed, leaning back, and slipping the stopper back into its place. He sighed again, patting his little round belly affectionately and smiling—a professional smile, Slocum decided.

"I'm not looking for a job," Slocum said, ignoring the glass of brandy that his host had placed on the side of the desk near him.

"This is not a regular job, however." Undershaft held up his hand to fend off any objection. "Let me tell you what it is. It's simply—well, in one sense, it's simple. To be sheriff of Hardtown, including a sizeable chunk of territory between here and Flint Butte to the north, and Rattle River south and east—I'm giving you a rough sketch—and west to about the Sunset Rimrocks. That's a pretty fair-sized territory, but not too many outfits. See, the chances are about one hundred to nothing that Hardtown's going to become county seat. Of course, that's not final yet. But it looks good. Fact, it looks very good. Like a cigar?" And he reached to a box on the desk.

Slocum said nothing as Undershaft placed the fine Havana cigar on the desk beside his glass.

"The pay would be good, Slocum. Very good. And of course any old scores that one might have from the past could easily be settled, or let's say explained, through the fact of having been working with the law."

"The past?"

"Any misunderstandings, you see. One can explain a lot by simply claiming—and being able to prove—that one was working let's say under cover for the law. I can have it arranged, you see, that you were already working with us during the past, let's say three, four months."

Slocum had to restrain the grin that suddenly wanted to spring into his face, but he managed to remain stern as he said, "But how do you get a man to be sheriff without an election? A marshal, all right. You can rig an appointment in the right quarters. But a sheriff has to be elected. I'm only asking out of curiousity; I'm not at all interested in taking the job."

"Of course." Undershaft struck the wooden lucifer and lighted his cigar, sending a stream of blue smoke toward the ceiling of the room.

It smelled wonderful to Slocum and his eyes dropped to the cigar Undershaft had given him.

"Light up," said his host.

"Well, it's of no great importance. I know you can get about anything you want if you go about it in a certain way," Slocum said, still ignoring the offer.

"It would be simple. First of all it would have nothing to do with an election. Buck Charles is sheriff, and he appoints you deputy. Charles gets sick, has to retire, and he appoints you to be acting sheriff until an election. The election can then come . . ." He waved a hand, "on doomsday."

Slocum nodded. He'd already figured it out, but he'd wanted Undershaft to say it.

"So what you want actually is a regulator, working for the law on the face of it, but actually working for you."

Undershaft was beaming. "Precisely. A good deal of the work would consist of observing what goes on."

"Spying."

"If you like to put it that way, all right then." Undershaft took a pull at his drink. "You see, a good bit of your surveillance would be taking place around Carter Mountain. That's Miner Creek north of here, and it's a big section of land with four ranches, including one outfit that I believe you're acquainted with." He smiled, savoring his score.

"What's at Prairie Dog?" Slocum asked suddenly. And he saw that his question was not expected, for Undershaft gave just the slightest reaction, covering it with a cough, holding his fist against his mouth, then feeling his crisp mustache with the tips of his fingers.

"Ah, yes . . . Prairie Dog. Matter of fact, I was about to bring up that subject. You realize that Prairie Dog is roughly within the Carter Mountain section. In other words, it would be within your purview."

"Not mine, Undershaft."

But the other man swept on, ignoring the objection. "And thus would be a place needing close surveillance." He hunched forward a little, elbows on the arms of his chair, his palms flat together as in prayer, their edges touching his face. "Hmmm. That is the, shall we say, center or headquarters— yes, that's a better word—the headquarters of one of the most clever and successful aggregates of criminal talent in the whole of the West, the frontier."

"What is their chief stock in trade?" Slocum asked innocently.

"Horses, cattle, gambling, gulling the rubes any way they can, theft, even murder. They're a very, very rough bunch." He paused. "But I would expect you—providing you accept this assignment—simply to watch, to observe." He lifted his glass. "It's good brandy, Slocum." And his eyes fell on his guest's untouched drink. "But look . . ." He put his glass down and leaned onto his forearms, his eyes directly on Slocum. "You see, I know you know the law. The regular legal lawmen can't cope with outlaws. The star restricts a good man more than it helps him. Why do you suppose so many stockmen hire private lawmen, regulators? Men who have a freer hand and aren't tied, bound by legal tape. A regulator, like a stock detective who is hired privately, he can come and go. Nobody knows he's a lawman. Or, if they do, they're more apt to obey him than the legal lawman because they know he doesn't have to follow the rules so closely. I know you understand me, Slocum."

Slocum said nothing, but kept his eyes on the other man, quietly observing his face, his breathing, what was going through him. He could see that he was making Undershaft ·just a little uneasy, though not throwing him by any means.

Undershaft leaned onto his forearms again, the tip of his tongue touching his upper lip. "Frankly, Slocum, what is needed is a peacemaker. A strong man with the law in his heart. A man who cannot be bought! A man who holds to his word, who can handle a gun, and who isn't against dealing with trouble, and maybe also having some fun on the side." He paused. "I can see what you're thinking. That I want someone in office who I can manipulate. It's the exact opposite, Slocum. I assure you!" He held up a restraining palm, though Slocum hadn't stirred either to move or speak. He took a short drink and, lowering his glass, said, "You see, you can do the job with or without the star, as you feel the need in the particular situation. Consider it! It's going to work beautifully. You'd be like a monitor. A much-needed help to this community, which at present is under siege from gangs of rustlers, horse thieves, murderers, and God knows what else. I know, for instance, about the men who tried to set fire to the DV. And if you hadn't been there?" He slapped the palm of his hand down on the desk. "What would have happened to those women, let alone the property and the stock!"

Slocum was on his feet. "It's not my line of work, mister."

"Let me tell you something, Slocum. People here in town know you. Some of them heard you were headed this way. Did you know that?"

"How did they know it, that's the question," Slocum said. And he stood firmly in front of the desk. "How did anyone know I was heading toward Hardtown, and what difference would it make to anyone?"

"Please sit down. Take a drink. Smoke. I want to talk to you. I promise I won't be long." And Undershaft smiled.

"I'm a busy man," Slocum said. "I can give you a few more minutes."

"Listen. There are people here who have heard of you, who admire you, and they are people who want a strong man to stand in the boots of the law and help the town grow. To make Hardtown grow, by George!"

"But how, why, do they see me like that? And how did they know I was coming here? How come they've got all built up on how great I am!" He snorted. "As if I didn't know—huh!"

Undershaft was almost grinning. Slocum took note of the slight space between his two upper front teeth that gave him the appearance of a mischievous boy.

"Yes, you guessed it. But not only from me. From the grapevine, the grubline gossip, whatever they call it. Slocum, you have to realize that to a number of people you are already a hero of the frontier, a man of action who brooks no nonsense from the criminal element. I was watching the scene in The Best Time while you were there. I saw the way some of them looked at you. And I had a report on it, too. Not from Charles only, but two others."

Slocum started to walk to the door.

"But you haven't had your drink!" insisted Undershaft. "Or your cigar! Why not hear me out? Sit down. Please! Slocum, I am pleading! Something I never, never, never do! Hear me out! First of all, I can inform you on anything you want to know about this country. I know that you cannot have ridden here simply because of the trouble with Captain Simmers's vigilantes!"

Slocum stood stock still, glaring at the other man. "I see. So you know about Simmers."

"I have my ways."

"I'll bet you do."

"Simmers and his associates have no notion that you're here in Hardtown."

"I know I could bet on that, Undershaft."

"I am glad that we finally begin to understand each other, Slocum." He coughed into the back of his hand. "Now then, as a former and even sometimes present preacher, let me say that I am rather good at reading crowds, their attitudes, their facial and verbal expressions. I've made a study of it. And I don't regret a minute of that unremitting labor. It has paid off handsomely. Thus, I consider myself rather an expert not only on reading crowds, but individuals, and I am telling you that you can have the people of this small community in the palm of your hand. Indeed, it is already so. As a veteran in the field, I can tell you I have learned of the power that lies in a man who is trusted by the multitude." He paused, but briefly, for a drink. Then resumed.

"I saw clearly how the crowd responded to you in The Best Time. You may think you don't have them in the palm of your hand, Slocum, but I assure you that you do."

"And Charles played his part well then, I see."

"Admirably. I rehearsed him many, many times."

"For Chrissake, Undershaft, not a one of them ever set eyes on me before today. They don't know me from Wild Bill Hickok!"

"But they will, Slocum. And right now they know what they *want* to know. I assure you—yes, I can see in your face that you understand—I assure you that Charles and I have not been idle in this matter. Myself, of course, principally!" Suddenly, he whipped out a big blue bandanna from a hip pocket and wiped his forehead, neck, chin, and face. "Now I must warn you. You have in your hands a public trust. They want you. They will even see you as their savior." A rich chuckle suddenly burst from him. He put away the bandanna and smoothed his mustache with his fingertips.

"So I see Rabbit Rock finally did follow me here," Slocum said ruefully.

Royal Undershaft beamed at him. "Such is fame, my friend. Such is the demand for a good man in this poor day and age."

"I'll turn it over," Slocum said as he turned back to the door.

"No drink? No cigar?"

He shook his head.

"Don't want to compromise yourself, eh? Well . . ." He let it hang.

Slocum had reached the door, his thoughts churning with how Undershaft had planned the whole deal, long before he, Slocum, had even thought of leaving Rabbit Rock. The man was sharp, and that was for sure. And he played all the angles, covered everything.

He realized now, as he paused at the door, that Undershaft, though a man of tremendous pride, would go to any lengths to gain his point. Even to put himself in jeopardy. That is, he would even risk his self-respect. Yes, Slocum was sure of that. He looked back at the man at the desk who was still standing there with his fingers spread apart as he leaned lightly onto some scattered papers.

Yes, any lengths.

5

Sure enough, Slocum spotted the busted-up derby hat within five minutes after leaving Royal Undershaft's office. Plain as his own hand, directly across the street, and under it the familiar, ugly face of— he didn't know the name—a Simmers lieutenant.

It wasn't even necessary to remind himself how well he had covered his backtrail; to no purpose evidently, for they'd somehow found out— or Undershaft had told them—where he was. They'd simply ridden a different trail to the place they knew he was heading for. Strange, how that nagging feeling had been with him all along that something was out of kilter. One thing was very clear: that Undershaft had been on his trail this good while.

He continued down the street, on the lookout for any others of the gang, but if there were any, they were keeping out of sight. He probably could expect a visit, though he figured they would wait a bit to see whether or not he accepted Undershaft's offer.

Entering the Smith Hotel, he put Undershaft out of his mind for the moment and signed the register for a room.

"You want with or without," the clerk asked.

He was a boy in his teens with slicked-down hair and was obviously holding down the desk for the regular clerk.

"With . . . ?" Slocum's thought had centered on a bath in the usual galvanized iron tub, with hot water brought in with a kettle.

"With someone," the boy said. "Or is it just you want the room for yerself?"

Slocum had grinned then, getting it, and realizing the boy had been instructed in just how to speak to him.

"Without," he said. "I generally pick my own company."

"Yessir," the boy said, and sniffed, trying to look older than he actually was.

The room was at the front of the building overlooking the main street. Again Slocum wondered how it was that a man of Undershaft's obvious abilities would be spending his time in such a backwater.

He lay down on the cornhusk mattress, the bed creaking loudly, and went over the situation that had so suddenly confronted him. Not only the meeting with Dolly Dolores and her lovely sister, but Undershaft and his whole deal. It was a helluva note, he decided. Dammit, it was bad enough when a man got marked as a top gun and a bunch of crazy challengers kept showing up to kill him to prove he wasn't.

Well, no matter. Undershaft was for sure not a

man to stand around with the grass growing under him. He played a big hand, and he held his cards close to his vest. Only why had he picked John Slocum? He was clearly no fool, but he should have known better. Something told Slocum that Undershaft had known very well why he was picking Mister John Slocum; Slocum was indeed a top gun, but he was also a straightshooter and didn't go point blank against the law. Sure there'd been misunderstandings now and again, but no big action. And too, he wasn't so publicly known as men like Hickok, Curly Bill, or the Earps.

He must have dozed off, for the next thing he knew he was wide awake, catching the quiet knock at the door of his room. In a trice, he was on his feet, his hand on the butt of the Colt sidearm which never moved very far from wherever he happened to be.

"Who is it?" His words coincided with a second knocking.

"Room service." The voice was muffled.

He was still fully on guard, standing to the side of the door, with the Colt in his right hand, reaching over with his left to turn the key.

"I'm Rosalie," the blonde said as she walked somewhat warily into the room, with her large eyes on the gun in Slocum's fist. Her red satin gown looked as though she had grown it as a second skin, revealing every curve, every softness, even her quick breathing. He found her smile delightful, partly bold but not without a charming shyness.

"Mister Undershaft said you might want some company." Her grey eyes turned up at the corners.

"And the room clerk?" Slocum asked, stepping back a little so as not to appear rude by holding her in the doorway.

"Johnnie? He said you told him you didn't want company, but we thought you might maybe change your mind."

"We?"

A second voice floated in, followed by its owner.

"I'm Kate. Rosalie and I like to work together. But of course that's up to you, Mister Slocum."

Slocum could do nothing but stare. The second girl who now appeared was absolutely identical with the first, even to the same red satin gown.

His jaw fell. "You're sisters."

"Twins," Rosalie said.

"Identical," said Kate.

Slocum had stepped back into the room. "You look like the spittin' image . . ." He couldn't take his eyes off them.

"You can't tell us apart," said the one named Kate. "Not even our parents could."

"You mean . . ." he almost blurted. "You mean *everything*? *Everything* is identical?"

"There's a way to find out," Rosalie said. At least Slocum thought it was Rosalie speaking. He wasn't really sure any longer who was who.

But he pulled himself together and said, "Ladies, you're both lovely, but you see, I've made it a rule never to pay for it."

"Don't worry," said one—he was no longer sure, but thought it was Rosalie. Ah yes, it was; the red dress was just a little looser than Kate's.

"Oh, I wasn't worrying about it."

They were both well inside the room now, and

Kate had closed the door gently behind her.

"You see," Rosalie said, "Mister Undershaft has taken care of all that."

"That's real good of the old boy," Slocum said.

"Mister Undershaft is a kind and generous man," Kate said as she sat down on the edge of the bed.

"I would like you girls to make yourselves at home," Slocum said drily. "But it just so happens I am busy at the moment. So I'm going to have to ask you to leave."

"But wouldn't you like to find out what our difference is?" asked the one he thought was Kate.

"You mean there's a way to tell?"

They turned toward each other and burst out laughing. "Of course," they both said in unison, "but it's ours to know and yours to find out."

Slocum couldn't hold back the grin at this point. "Mister Undershaft doesn't happen to be Greek does he?"

"Greek?" They looked at each other in surprise. "We dunno. Maybe. But why? What does it matter."

Slocum had walked to the door and opened it. "You've not heard the expression, Beware of Greeks bearing gifts?"

They looked at him in silence. Then again looked at each other, each raising her eyebrows in surprise and giving a little shrug.

"Girls, ladies, I'm sorry, but in matters of sex and in fact in matters of everything I make it a habit, a rule, that I make the decisions."

They stared at him, as though they couldn't believe what they were hearing.

Once again they turned toward each other,

opened their arms and shrugged.

"You're missing something, mister," one of them said. Kate? Rosalie? While the other—Rosalie? Kate? nodded in vigorous agreement.

"I know. But so are you."

"Hah!" This exclamation came from both of them simultaneously.

"Mister Undershaft has good taste, I will say that for him," Slocum said, smiling as they went out the door. "So long."

He went out for a walk then, and when he returned to his room he could still smell the odor of their perfume, just lightly. He knew very well then what he was going to do. He remembered what he had said to the girls about Greeks bearing gifts, but there was also the old saying about not looking a gift horse in the mouth.

After all, business needn't necessarily interfere with pleasure, and Mister Undershaft looked to be intelligent enough to get the message. Besides, there should be at least one other saying about business and pleasure, or anyway about pleasure. Anyway, doing it was what was important—not remembering what some wise apple said about it.

"I have got to say, I can't see even an inch of difference, even a shadow, in you ladies."

They were standing in front of him stark naked, only their stance was slightly different—one stood swing-hipped, the other on her toes with one foot crossed in front of the other, like a dancer.

Slocum was sitting on the edge of the big double bed with his erection thrust into the air. He was wearing only his shirt.

"You know we're going against house rules," Rosalie said. He knew it was Rosalie because she'd told him, and she was wearing a ring on her little finger for identification.

"Sorry, but I told you I don't believe in paying for it." He held up his hand to stem any objection. "However, I don't mind giving you ladies a gift later, if you've no objection. But I never pay for sex."

"A gift?" Rosalie looked at her sister. "Money?"

"Maybe," Slocum said. "Maybe not. But of course that depends on the quality of the goods."

"You drive a hard bargain, mister."

"That's right," he said, looking down at his erection. "And there he is."

"He's cute," Kate said. "What do you say, Roe? Want to go along with it?"

"We don't understand why you didn't want Mister Undershaft to pay for it. That way you'd have gotten it free. Now, like this, you'd still be paying, even though you say you don't ever pay for it. You give us a gift, that's payment."

"Not like this. If I give you a gift—and I might not, see—it's because I like you and might have been giving you something anyway."

While they were talking, standing there totally naked, they were each eyeing his erect member, hardly able to drag their eyes away from it.

"Oh, to hell with it," Rosalie said and dropped down onto her knees, grabbing his cock in her hand and guiding it to her eager mouth.

Slocum lay back, quivering with desire as she sucked him in long, even strokes.

In the meantime, Katie had come onto the bed on her knees and with one hand was guiding her right nipple into his mouth.

"Suck it," she said. "I love it so . . ."

With his other hand he was reaching down to take her sister's left tit as she licked his long shaft, fluttering it with her tongue till he thought he'd lose his mind.

"Who you going to give it to?" one of them gasped in his ear as they changed positions, with Rosalie bring her teat to his mouth and Katie going down on him.

Slocum could hardly bear it. He was gasping. "Surprise me," he managed to say. "But God, one of you get on him."

And all at once he rolled over on top of—he didn't know who—and mounted her high and hard and deep. While from behind him her sister held his balls in her hand, tickling and squeezing while he rode the bucking girl beneath him deeper and higher and faster as the two of them squealed and whimpered with joy and Slocum thought he would lose his mind. Whoever was fondling his balls squeezed ever so gently, just the right strength as he rode her sister higher and faster and deeper as both girls cried out in their exquisite happiness and Slocum came and came and came . . .

John Slocum was a man mostly used to his own company. He didn't favor crowds and, for the most part, stayed away from the big towns such as Cheyenne, Denver, Dodge, and Ellsworth. Though there had been moments in his life when he had decided on a change and had spent time in Kansas City, Laramie, and Frisco, but never for very long.

In eluding the posse from Rabbit Rock, he had

thought that it might be a good thing to hole up for a spell in one of the larger towns, the kind a man could get lost in. But as he'd come further north and had begun to feel the high country more, his mood had changed, and he felt an old longing for the mountains. Sure, you could get lost in a big town where there were lots of people. But in places like that, soldiers could be a problem. They came to the army from all over, with a likelihood that one of them might have seen a dodger on him or maybe even remembered or heard something about him that would better have been forgotten.

The fact was the West was a hive of gossip, most of it untrue, as was the nature of gossip, yet carrying enough that had actually happened so that there was damage nonetheless. In any event, he preferred the smaller towns or solitude. He liked his own company.

These reflections had been in his mind as he'd ridden away from Rabbit Rock, dodging the posse. Now, having stumbled on Dolly Dolores VanDam and her delightful sister, he was simply damn glad to be wherever it was he found himself at whatever time.

Glad to be where he was. At the same time, he realized he didn't want any part of Royal Undershaft, Buck Charles, or the job offered him.

No question, Undershaft was the type who could slicker the drawers off a nun in less time than it took a cat to lick its own ass. As he rode slowly along the winding trail, Slocum reviewed the situation that had taken place in Hardtown, fitting it to Rabbit Rock and Captain Simmers's vigilantes.

Undershaft had come right out with it finally, as Slocum, leaving the office, had paused with his hand on the doorknob.

Slocum had seen it coming for a mile, could feel the man winging into the clincher, knew all along what he was going to say long before he heard the words.

"Rabbit Rock." Those two words, dropping from those thin lips were like a pair of spade aces, and Slocum knew he was in a bind for sure.

Undershaft had been grinning at him over his glass of brandy, through the thick smoke of his goddamn cigar.

The voice had extra gravel in it. "Interesting place, Rabbit Rock, I never been there, that part of the country, but I've got friends—well, maybe not exactly friends, but men I do business with . . ." The last two words were left hanging in the cigar smoke, the odor of brandy, the stuffiness of the room. "They—uh—recommended you as a man I could depend on."

Slocum had felt a little tightening, followed by the instant loosening at the warning from his body. Of course, the whole game had been a setup through Simmers so that the sonofabitch could rope him into his scheme, whatever that was.

Undershaft's small eyes had suddenly disappeared into his flat cheeks, as a rich chuckle fell from his lips. "Ah, I knew they were singing the right song, Mister Slocum. I'm a very good judge of men, as you may or may not yet realize. My friends, or rather, I should say my associates in the Rabbit Rock area, knew just the kind of man I needed for my extremely important assignment. I know you will appreciate the care, the fine planning that is going into the work, or at least you will as things develop. And surely by then you will appreciate just why I have chosen you for the—uh—special assignment I have in mind."

At this point Slocum had turned back to the door. "So long, mister. I am not interested."

Undershaft didn't even blink. The tone of voice was dry as a bleached bone. "Mister Slocum, how can you be so foolish as to turn down my offer? I mean to say, with a not small posse virtually breathing down the back of your neck."

Slocum had stopped with one foot almost on the other side of the doorway. "Mister, you and your vigilante friends can go piss up a rope."

The grin that had started on Undershaft's face broadened. "Capital!" His large teeth seemed to spring right out of his mouth as the grin got even bigger. "Capital!" He repeated the word.

"Slocum, you are behaving as I had expected; with the colors of a truly independent man. A man of courage, force, enterprise, and a full sense of your own worth. That is precisely why you are so necessary to my work, sir. And as I say, I admire wholeheartedly your independence. All the same, sir, I must insist. You see, if you refuse me, then I have only one choice."

"Sic the posse on me. So . . ."

"Of course," Undershaft said agreeably, "but then you might very well elude them again." He held up his hand to forestall any interruption as he swept on. "But you see, I know the circumstances of your entrapment by the men in Rabbit Rock. I arranged all that, you see. And believe me, it wasn't at all

easy. But you will have to admit, it was effective."
He waved a pudgy hand. "But go if you must. If
you insist."

And John Slocum picked up instantly on the devilish grin in Royal Undershaft's eyes as he added
with just the right edge to his words, "But then, of
course, I shall simply have to visit my old—well,
let me say former—acquaintance, Dolly Dolores
VanDam, for advice on what to do with a recal-
citrant male. Dolly is an expert in such matters.
And her, uh, sister . . . Well, I'm sure you catch my
drift, sir."

In that instant, Slocum felt something clutch
right in the center of his guts. Then he let it
go, saying, "You cover everything, don't you, you
sonofabitch."

Undershaft had the good sense not to grin, not
to crow, and to let Slocum's remark pass. "That's
what I've been telling you, old boy. Of course, Dolly isn't a close friend. Only a business associate.
You know how much information you can get in
a bedroom. Even more than with the bottle, if the
hand is well played. I'm sure you can appreciate
my insistence, Slocum. By the way I am happy
to see that her sister and she have finally gotten
together. Interesting, families. Wouldn't you say?
A lovely girl that young Sally."

Slocum, with his hand still close to the doorknob,
had turned more squarely toward the man at the
desk.

"You know, Undershaft, I think it would be a
good idea if you changed your name."

"Good heavens! Change my name? What ever
for?"

"In honor of the way you do business."

"And change it to what, if you don't mind my asking?"

"To Shaft," Slocum said. And with a hard grin etched on his face he walked out, closing the door behind him.

In the hot sun, the two men slugged wearily at each other. Neither could muster that extra something that could knock the other man down. Each seemed about ready to fall, but somehow managed to stay up.

"They're both done for, fer Chrissakes," growled a spectator. "Exceptin' they're too far gone to drop."

"Dead, by God, but they won't lie down," observed another judicious spectator.

Even so, bets were still being taken as preparations went on for the expected horse racing that was coming up.

"C'mon! Finish him off, fer Chrissakes!" somebody shouted. "Let's get to the hosses!"

"Slam the sonofabitch, Billy Boy!"

"Himes, you dumb fuck, you couldn't fight yer way outta a wet paper bag!"

Indeed, all were impatient for the horse race to start. The fight was an impromptu affair. Interest in it had appeared with the indifference of the weather. Someone had insulted someone else, or at any rate had overstepped the mark of accepted social grease maintained for the particular milieu. Honor, real or imagined, was at stake.

The action was at Prairie Dog, otherwise known in that part of the country as Stone-Hole-in-the-Wall. It was in this fortified stone castle that the

Bart Gooden boys holed up, rested, and cavorted between their hard work, while their leader—it was said in utmost secrecy—counted the money and planned their future activities.

It was a good life, no question. Any one of the men present would surely have agreed. The "roost", a name by which the Hole was also known, consisted of several cabins or shacks and a makeshift saloon and gambling establishment; that is, there were card tables, chairs, and dice tables. Now and again there was music, depending on the presence of personnel who could scratch the fiddle. And there were girls.

The hideout was—as a newspaper reporter had once described it—virtually inaccessible. Several lawmen had recently failed in a combined effort to bring the Gooden gang to book. They had failed miserably, retreating with their ranks decimated, and no one had tried a further assault. It was understood that once inside the first box canyon that formed the chain of hidden and most dangerous traps for any interloper, a visitor had about the chance of a fart in hell. For sure, no lawman had ever found his way out of the maze of box canyons. Indeed, so vigorous was the reputation of Prairie Dog and its leader that no one even made the attempt these days.

"Billy Boy looks to be about ready to toss it in," someone in the crowd observed. "Can't hardly lift his arms."

"Dumb shit should'na sounded off like he done."

"Himes ain't that much better off," another voice announced.

"I got five says Clem's first to go down."

"Fade ya," said a third voice.

Just then the man named Himes, hardly managing to stay on his feet, with blood streaming from his nose, one eye firmly buried under a black-and-blue lump, hardly able to lift his battle-weary arms, summoned some miraculous force from who knew where and drove a smashing right to the side of Billy Bannister's big head, landing right on the temple, and dropping his opponent to the hard ground like a pole-axed steer. But his punch had taken everything he had, including what strength he needed to stay on his feet, and in the next instant, he staggered, spun almost halfway around and fell right on top of his prone adversary.

"They both of 'em is out!" somebody shouted and let out a Texas yell.

"The hell you say!" barked the man who had bet on Billy.

"By God, I do say!" yelled the man who had claimed a draw. "All bets is off!"

"Himes cold-cocked the sonofabitch!" The voice rose as rage supplanted initial irritation and then anger. "Himes was longest on his feet, by God!"

"It's a double knockout," somebody said. "Nobody's winner."

At this point, Harelip Thoms began to say something, but since his physical difficulty made it almost impossible for people ever to understand him, nobody was even trying to listen.

"Shut it!"

These hard words, sounding like the crack of a pair of bullets, came from Bart Gooden, who until then had remained silent, simply watching the fight, listening casually to the betting, the chattering of the men, but as he usually did, keeping apart, aloof, with a good attention on what was taking place around him.

It was the annoying thing about him. The men hated it—his eyes and ears on them. "Like a fucking mother, fer Chrissakes," someone had put it. Some, like the two Harrigan boys, had almost given life to the words, though never within Mister Gooden's hearing. The terrible thing was, you never had a moment to yourself. He was always onto you, listening, watching, while he chewed or smoked or drank or was just there breathing.

"Man can't take a leak, can't fart without him bein' onto it," someone pointed out one time.

"Man cain't scratch his own ass," another said in support of that statement. Unfortunately, he was overheard, and his boss had instantly dropped him with a savage rabbit punch, a wicked blow delivered from the rear, and the victim had lain as though dead.

There had been a number of witnesses to this graceful conclusion to that conversation, but no one spoke, no one moved to assist the fallen outlaw.

"Reckon that'll learn ya who does the scratchin' around here," Bart Gooden had said with a wicked grin. "Huh!" And he had punctuated this remark with a thick stream of brown and yellow saliva, shot with perfect accuracy onto a small lizard who was on its way to the shelter of a clump of sagebrush.

"By God, I do believe the man ain't with us no more," he went on, cocking a professional look at the limp body at his feet. "Shit, reckon he can take up permanent residence here with the law."

This sally brought forth a round of laughter, reminding the boys of how not so long back a lawman had indeed breached the maze of box-canyon defenses and even a couple of outriders and had made it to the center of the Prairie Dog hideout, where he was greeted by none other than Bart Gooden himself.

"What kin I do for ya, mister?" Bart had asked, with a wicked grin streaking his hairy jowels.

"Just wanted to have a look-see," the deputy had replied. "Name's Foley. Tad Foley, out of Cheyenne. I'd heard you didn't have no permanent law in Prairie Dog, and when I spoke to my superior, I was ordered to investigate. See how it was. Like the why and how of it."

This had brought a sparkle into Mister Gooden's eyes, and he had looked around at the group of men standing in a rough semi-circle observing their visitor.

"Reckon you feel pretty neat finding us so easy-like," Bart had said, with a wink in the direction of his men. "Sorry to disappoint you. Fact is, we do indeed have a permanent lawman right here in Prairie Dog."

"I was told you didn't. 'Leastways, not permanent."

"You was told correct, young feller. We didn't. We didn't useter have a permanent lawman, just one that showed up now and again like. Casual, see. Not permanent. But now we do."

And suddenly that big sixgun had been in Bart Gooden's fist, and he had shot that deputy dead.

Holstering slick as grease, his chuckle was rich.

"And you, you be him, mister."

And this sample of frontier humor had brought the gang to the ground with mirth. The Permanent Law was buried forthwith, and a wood headpiece was planted right over the spot. On it a hot running iron usually used for altering brands burned the statement: "Permanent Law come to Prairie Dog this day. Stranger, you be standing on it." Followed by the date.

Bart Gooden was feeling good. Pretty damn good for the matter of that, he was telling himself as he strolled about the encampment that was now almost a town—indeed was a town, thanks to himself. Formerly nothing but hardpan and scrubby sage, there now stood a number of cabins—a few of logs, more of sod that had been packed in on horses, and one of lumber stolen from the railroad. The frame house was, of course, Bart Gooden's. There stood also, though Bart Gooden would have worded it differently, life where before there had been no human hand. There was a life and an activity that said "town". He saw it again, he felt it, and he felt good about it as he strolled, with thumbs hooked into his wide leather belt, with the brace of Colts riding on his thick hips. And all this, all of it, defined his purpose. Indeed, himself.

He paused, taking out a wooden lucifer and began picking his teeth. He listened to the voices of the men some yards away from him as they set up for the horse racing. Besides the fun of the race, there was another purpose at hand, which was to test a number of the ponies that had been brought in, checking their good and bad points. Later, they would have fresh markings applied that would be so well done they would defy identification even by their legitimate owners.

Bart Gooden smiled at how easy everything was going. Besides horseflesh, there was cattle, a large band of which had been run in the night before and were so trail-toughened that they were practically jerked beef on the hoof. But they were meat, and he knew that his best ticket for the coming winter was going to be the ability to supply Hardtown and the army with prime beef. Not to forget booze.

Cattle and the constant turnover of horses made the mare go, as the saying had it. Brought the money in. The boys, plus anyone who leased their horses, were sure not to be traced through their mounts, especially with the good paintwork on the markings. After a job, everything was washed off with turpentine.

It was a perfect setup. Range Delaney had proved himself unusually adept at handling horses, so for the purposes of giving a legitimate front to the enterprise, the head man had asked Bart to appoint him as horse buyer for Prairie Dog Ranch. Delaney had traveled as far east as Kansas in his hunt for fast horses, and with the head man's backing to help him in bargaining, he usually managed to come back to Prairie Dog with the best.

These would then be sold to the carriage trade in and around Hardtown, and also in Tensleep, Crayton, and Sand Butte, but not until they had been used at least once to hold up a stage.

And the enterprise was expanding. Indeed, the head man—Mister Undershaft—hardly talked of anything else nowadays. Clearly he had something further on his mind. Something big. It was a gut. The man was always coming up with something, some new way to skin a cat. Like the horses, then the cattle, then the stage jobs—Lander, Miller Creek, Pitchfork, and them others. Then, well, that other business. Even though Bart Gooden wasn't sure what it was, he could smell it. He knew in his blood that this time the head man was up to something real big. The railroad was it? A bank? Bart wasn't sure. But he did feel the head man might be pushing too far this time. Just a feeling in his bones. He, Bart Gooden, was a straight one; he knew where to draw the line.

All the same, Undershaft said that whatever it was had to be. Or rather, he didn't actually say so in words. He did what he always did: he assumed that you'd go along with it. That was his way, and it was not for Bart Gooden to argue with the man. Undershaft knew some things about him that he wished he didn't.

Thing was, a man had to take care of himself. If you didn't see to yourself, then who would? Simple as dropping off a log, by God!

Likely the man might start going after the express cars, the railroad. Plenty of action there! That would be more like it. But as far as he could see, Undershaft wasn't thinking only along such lines. Well, maybe he'd find out at the meeting. Maybe something would come up then.

He had crossed to the north side of the big round horse corral, and now he stood looking at the dozen horses with new markings. He would examine each one more closely before he let the animals pass. Burt and Caine were good at their work, though not all that good that you could let 'em have their head. He'd caught a mistake last time and one time before, too. Hell, a man couldn't be too careful in this line of work. He'd have to crack down. Might bring this up at the meeting. Get in a good word for himself to boot.

6

On a particular morning about a month before the famous trial in Hardtown's Best Time Saloon, when the offices of the Denver Chronicle had opened, the little pudgy man in charge of the newspaper's morgue had looked toward the knock on his door and had been greeted by the smiling face of a tall, wiry man with a mass of white hair above a pink, burnished face that pointed down into a neat and very white goatee. He could smell the pomade, and he appreciated the clear blue, innocent-looking eyes of the stranger.

"I was wondering," said Elihu Lincoln Thong, placing his spotless derby hat on the official's desk, "if I might take a look at some of your back issues? I am preparing a long and very thorough article for a national publication and require a careful perusal of some of your work in order to have my facts and figures absolutely correct." These words were accompanied by a charming smile, one of Elihu Thong's best, a slightly obsequious bend of the head, a light lifting of the hand as though in payment for having possibly caused some inconvenience in the request, and a trace of a lesser smile at the corners of the eyes, all contributing to mollify the stern figure at the desk. It worked. For Elihu was a master of his craft and knew a rube when he saw one.

During the following week, Elihu steeped himself in every scrap of information he could find concerning what had been accomplished by the James and Burrows gangs, as well as a number of other train robbers. The plan, of course, was simply to do it better. And the newspaper accounts were a text on the methods.

At the same time, he took in the fact that Jesse's eventual downfall lay in his not knowing when to quit. Elihu had discovered this morsel of applied philosophy during his youth, when he watched a brood sow eat herself to death on his first employer's ranch. Jesse, too, had run a good thing too far for his own good, with the result that the railroad companies banded together and built a $10,000 reward for his capture dead or alive. The offer was irresistible, and Bob Ford copped it.

But now, to Elihu Lincoln Thong's thinking, the railroads and Pinkertons likely wouldn't yell too much if one, two, even three or four express cars were knocked off. In time, the headlines would fade, the Wanted posters would disappear in the wind, and people would do what they always did—they would forget.

In the late fall, after tutoring his group, which he had selected with care, Elihu decided that it would be a good moment to tackle the Forbes Express job, which he had selected as their first training exercise.

Their hit, he informed the boys, would have to take place somewhere outside St. Louis so that the Pinkertons, railroad bulls, and sheriffs wouldn't get suspicious and beef-up protection on the swift San Francisco overnight flyer to Springfield, Missouri, which would be their next— and much more serious—target. The first job was a complete success.

And so it happened that a couple of weeks later, a Missouri Pacific train was stopped by four men just outside Omaha. In no more than ten minutes, the safe in the Pacific Express Company car was relieved of $2,000.

It presently came to Elihu Thong's ears that Bill Pinkerton, stationed at Pinkerton's Midwestern Division office in Chicago, was irritated and yet somewhat amused as he read the messenger's report. The leader of the bandits was described as tall, thin, very well-dressed in a dark suit, with his white hair hardly hidden beneath his spotless derby hat. And for a moment Mister Pinkerton had considered that it all might have been some part of an involved joke. A derby hat! And spotless to boot!

But he was not amused for long. Ten days later, another report was handed in. The Milwaukee–St. Paul train had been stopped just outside Minneapolis by four men wearing masks. They had skillfully blown the express car apart with at least six sticks of dynamite. And one member of the gang was wearing a derby.

In result of this foray, the express messenger lay dying and the four train robbers had made off with $10,000. The man with the derby was leading the way.

Not bad—$12,000 in two weeks. And there was no doubt in Pinkerton's mind that the bandits were the same in both cases.

It had been enough for Elihu, his point being to prove that he could indeed outsmart, outgame even the Pinkerton Agency in a field that was only distantly related to his customary stamping ground— the card table, dice, betting, shilling, carnival barking, and most especially, gulling the rubes.

He was reflecting on all this riding his buckboard, which had brought him all the way from Hardtown across the sparse mountainous terrain, the land hard, dry as sun-polished bone, to the sudden oasis of box canyons whose maze entombed the inhospitable community known as Prairie Dog.

He had been to Prairie Dog before, in fact had spent a couple of days and nights exhibiting how to work the cards and dice to a tidy profit. This venture at teaching had been at the request of Royal Thor Undershaft and had been necessarily supported by Bart Gooden.

He was greeted, more or less, by none other than Mister Gooden himself.

"Made it . . ." Gooden let fly a streak of tobacco juice that dampened a fair piece of sagebrush as he stood swing-hipped, his fingers in his hip pockets, his head canted toward his visitor. "See you come back for seconds, huh."

Elihu, smooth as a drink of mountain water, allowed a grin to appear in his blue eyes. "Come to

listen to the palaver," he said. "Friend Undershaft
sent me a note. It appears he has need. Needs my
help, my expertise."

"Your what?" Bart dug himself into the hard
ground and glared at the strange words that came
from the visitor. "Better speak English 'round this
here, mister, if'n you fancy anybody to cotton to
what yer sayin'."

Elihu's grin broadened. He had no illusions about
the man he was facing. Gooden was a known killer, vicious and highly effective. No man to mess
with. But Thong wasn't stepping back. He could
be right up front with the likes of Bart Gooden—
that is, until it developed into hot-lead time. Thing
was not to allow anything to get that far. Elihu
Lincoln Thong had spent almost his entire life
learning assiduously how to out-think, outsmart,
out-maneuver anyone. After all, it was his career.

"Undershaft here?" he asked without taking his
eyes off the other man.

"He just come in past the first outrider," Bart
Gooden said, his words dry as the hot sage surrounding them. "He'll be here directly." And he
nodded toward the cabin.

Elihu looked at the sky where he spotted a lone
eagle spanning the great vault of blue. It was himself, that eagle, a lone eagle. Always higher than
anyone else. But he didn't like the way Gooden
had pointed out that Undershaft had been that
close to him without his knowing it. Well, he sure
as hell had to be sharp. Gooden was like a goddam club, a battering ram, ramming his hard eyes
right into a man. On the other hand, Undershaft
was slick as a snake and just as trustworthy.

There would be plenty he'd have to watch. All the same, he was thinking as he started toward the cabin, and as one of the outriders came up on a big sorrel horse, all the same he'd have to play it damn close to his vest. He felt the old thrill running through him, that thrill that appeared like a light, searing him, the tougher, the more dangerous the game got.

Elihu almost gave himself away—but of course didn't, being a true Master of his craft—when Royal Thor Undershaft turned to Bart Gooden as they entered the room in the frame house and told him he could leave.

"I will be talking with Mr. Thong privately, Gooden. But I will appreciate your being at hand."

"Ya mean you want me to git," said Bart Gooden, and he was not smiling.

"Uh-huh." Undershaft nodded, without looking up from the paper he was holding in his hand.

Elihu, restraining his wish to break into a grin, simply sniffed, and without waiting to be asked, sat down in the chair at the side of Undershaft's desk.

As the door closed behind the disgruntled Bart Gooden, Undershaft lifted his eyes to his companion.

"I see that the Pinkertons are still in a quandary over those, uh, interesting adventures with their express cars. I'm sure you've been hearing news through whatever sources you command, Thong."

Elihu inclined his head, pursed his lips, and gently rubbed the tips of his fingers together, holding his hands close to his chest. A smile played in his blue eyes and at the corners of his mouth. Early in life he had toyed with the notion of becoming an actor. The stage had attracted him. Instead, he had joined a carnival as a pitchman. The choice, he told himself, had certainly been the right one. His present field was much more interesting than mere cavorting on a stage before an audience. As it was now, he could combine his bent for histrionics along with his hunger for adventure, excitement, thrill, and risk, inventing his own role as he went along.

"It must be clear to you," Undershaft continued, releasing a soft, very slight belch along with his words, "that Hardtown is growing by leaps and bounds." He cocked his head, an engaging look in his eyes and watched how the other man took it.

"Right on the barrel head, I'd allow," said Thong. "A dance waiting for the music is how I see it."

A chuckle tumbled out of Royal Undershaft's loose mouth and down his high chest. "I see you're a man after my own taste," he said and gave a quick smile, which almost instantly vanished into a frown. His wide brow now became seamless as he leaned forward with his elbows on the big desk. "Let us get to the point, Mister Thong."

"Them's my own feelin's per exactly," said Elihu Lincoln Thong.

Royal Thor Undershaft cleared his throat and ran his palm across his wide diaphragm. He could see that his visitor was not an easy man to undo. But he would be patient, sometimes these things took a little time. He had no doubt that he would soon find the right opportunity for putting the uppity Mr. Thong in his place. But he was careful enough to keep the smile on his face as he held these thoughts.

"You're new to Hardtown, Thong. You've been here but a short while, and even so, you managed that court case admirably, I must admit. I didn't attend the proceedings myself, business occupying me rather heavily at the time, but I have a complete report on your brief and your—uh—behavior. Satisfactory, sir! Highly satisfactory!" And he leaned back in his chair, holding both his palms flat on the desk.

"My middle name ain't Lincoln for nothin'," said Thong.

"A great legal mind."

"A great man all round, one could allow," said Thong.

Swiftly, Undershaft pulled the conversation back into his own park. "But you are yet new to Hardtown. Let me fill you in a bit. You'll see how it will help us to understand each other and the work that we're facing."

"Proceed, then," Thong said, and gave a heavy sigh.

Royal Undershaft thought it just a little too heavy, but let it pass.

Undershaft's throat resounded like a small load of pebbles being dropped into a wooden box. His Adam's apple pumped a couple of times. He cleared his throat again, less noisily this time. "You are of course well aware of how Virginia City came into its present capacity and, I can add, notoriety."

"Be deaf, dumb, and blind if I didn't," said Mister Thong agreeably, the smile never for an instant leaving his face.

"Silver, as you of course know," Undershaft went on, ignoring the undercurrent coming from the man seated across from him.

Suddenly he lifted his forefinger. "But realize this! The prosperity of the Comstock lode was not wholly in its mining. That is to say, there was and still is a fortune not just in the mines but in the ancillary—if I may borrow a legal term—the ancillary endeavors."

Elihu blinked. "I do like the way you come up on a point," he said. He nodded. "Proceed, sir!"

Undershaft ignored the interruption. "You are well aware of the fortune made by the railroad alone, not to forget the road building that required the very mountains to be blasted in order to make roads for the timber wagons hauling in fuel and mine timbers from beyond Lake Tahoe and Sierraville. And even while the roads were being blasted through, the timber companies were building flumes up to twenty miles long, costing up to $250,000."

"That's what I know," said Thong, slipping the words in fast in an effort to keep Undershaft mindful of who he was talking to: not some one-suspender hick!

But Undershaft was unstoppable. He loved to talk, relying on mass and speed to overwhelm a listener. All the same, Thong was adjusting to it. He hadn't been brought up in the carnival circuit learning nothing.

"Let me tell you about one case," Undershaft continued, his deep, plangent voice gripping the room. "In one case, just to get enough water to float timbers 16-inches square and 30-feet long down an eighteen-mile flume, a tunnel 2,100 feet long was driven through a mountain to tap a lake on the other side." Undershaft's forefinger stabbed the air like a flagpole. "They built steamboats on Lake Tahoe to tow log rafts across and even then the supply of lumber and timber could not keep equal to the demands of the mines!" He paused only to catch fresh breath. "Do you, can you, realize how many *other* professions had to be called in to be able to support the mining, the railroad, and all the rest of it! Think! Think of it, man!" He brought the flat palm of his pink hand down hard on the top of the desk. A pencil rolled over the edge and hit the floor. Neither man noticed it.

"I do," said Elihu Thong softly, his eyes intent on the excited man seated on the other side of the big desk.

"I do," Elihu repeated.

"I know you do," said Undershaft. "For I am well aware of the fact that you were there at the time." And he sat back and looked steadily into the middle distance.

"The point," said Elihu after a rather long moment.

"The point is crystal clear," said Undershaft. "The point, as you very well know, having been there yourself, and as I have already, rather copiously pointed out, sir, is that a sizeable fortune was reaped in the process."

"How'n hell can you rape a fortune, Undershaft? Mister—just riddle me this! *Rape* a fortune . . . !"

"Reap! I said *reap*, not rape!" The corners of Undershaft's mouth were wet with his excitement at being so idiotically misunderstood. "Those men *made* a fortune is what I'm saying!"

"Then whyn't you say so. Hell, I thought you said 'raped', an' I mean, how'n hell can you figger on doin' that!" And the old boy had lapsed swiftly into cow-country lingo as he enjoyed himself belaboring the point, hoping to undo Mr. Smart-Aleck Undershaft.

Except he couldn't. It was not possible, and to his regret he saw that this was so. All the same, he knew he would try again. And so, for that matter, did Mister Undershaft.

And indeed, Elihu Thong launched instantly into a rather long and detailed account of how he had attempted to bring an astounding suggestion to the authorities in Virginia City and the Comstock lode.

So numerous were the achievements of the mining, lumbering, and road-building groups that nobody thought it even humorous or strange when the suggestion came from Elihu Lincoln Thong himself that Virginia City could enjoy the same hours of sunlight as did Gold Hill on the other side of the Divide. Because Virginia City was on the east slope of Mount Davidson and the sun shone for two hours longer on the west slope, the proposal authored by Elihu Thong was that a tunnel be cut through the mountain to transmit the sunlight, which would then be distributed by a series of huge mirrors. Unfortunately, there was no apparent way in which any of the authorities or business folk could cash in on it. Even though Thong eloquently pointed out that the mirrors could be directed to shine only on those places that paid a handsome fee for those extra sunlight hours.

"A brilliant idea, I do agree with you, Thong."
Undershaft beamed as he said those words. "But
you see, impractical. In you sir, I see a man of true
genius. I happen to be blessed, or possibly cursed,
according to how you look at it, with the same
quality. But I, in distinction from yourself, sir,
have been blessed with a mind that includes total
practicality. You do not have that sort of thinking
apparatus, sir. Yet, I can use you for what you do
have. Am I making myself absolutely clear?"

"Hunh!" snorted Elihu, and he shifted in his
chair as though he was sitting on something
uncomfortable.

Undershaft swept on, noting his discomfort but
intent now on making his point. "I have admira-
tion, Thong, for certain of your talents. The suggestion about the mirrors is not included in that
summation. Rather, I am interested in the contacts
you have; that is to say, the contacts you have with
certain useful members of our community. Certain
members who have a talent such as the one you
showed me in regard to the aging of certain documents, and in certain legal aspects that can be put
to good account. I mean to say, for instance, that
the two men you sent to teach some of Gooden's
ruffians how to deal with horse markings were
good. Not very good," he added. "Simply good."

He stopped, reached down to the small cupboard
at the foot of his desk and returned with a decanter
of brown fluid.

"An excellent brandy. Join me."

Without further ado, there were two glasses on
the desk, and the genial host filled each with that
delicious liquid.

Undershaft released a great breath of air, the power of which, laced as it was with that powerful brandy, almost brought tears to the eyes of Elihu Lincoln Thong.

"You see, Thong, we of Hardtown can emulate such as Virginia City."

"Can't quite follow that word, Mister," said the old conman with a slow grin, though he knew perfectly well its meaning.

"I mean, I have a good use for you, you old bugger. Just remember—you understand?—just never forget that I know about Dodge and Kansas City."

A loud silence now fell into the room as Elihu shifted uncomfortably in his chair.

"I never had piles myself," Undershaft said with a face that would have disarmed an angel.

And Elihu Lincoln Thong would gladly have cut his throat from ear to ear.

Undershaft watched, lids at half mast, but missing not a thing. He was reading the whole story along with Thong, the man's history, his aliases, the railway hold-ups, the whole picture.

"What the hell do you want, Undershaft?"

"I want a gold mine."

"Jesus . . ."

"Jesus has nothing to do with it, my friend. Elihu Thong is the man who will get it for me."

"A gold mine?"

"Yup."

"Mind tellin' me how I'm gonna do this."

Royal Undershaft leaned forward heavily on his desk, on top of a couple of layers of papers, plans, letters, and two loose cigars that he had mislaid early in the day.

"It'll be the easiest thing in the world," Undershaft said, and he added, "my lad."

"Shit . . ."

"You will sell the idea of a gold strike in the same way that you began your career by selling patent medicines to the gulls." And he leaned forward onto the desk with all those papers, opening his palms toward the ceiling, with a broad smile on his face. "Nothing could be simpler."

"Huh!" snorted Elihu sitting upright in his chair. "And you think people won't cotton to that kind of slickering, do ya?"

Undershaft's smile broadened until it looked to Elihu as though it would connect his two ears.

"Friend, did anyone ever catch you gulling the rubes with that phoney patent medicine you used to make yourself?"

"I do believe I am beginning to get your notion there," Thong said, turning brisk. "You've in mind the digging on the other side of Carter Mountain."

"In a manner of speaking, yes." Undershaft's mouth twitched, as though he was trying not to grin.

"I see. You figger they'll think they can make it on this side."

"Do you? What it is necessary to see, my friend, is that you can only cheat a man who wants to be cheated. The rubes just feel that vein might just be extended." He chuckled. "Don'cha know . . ."

7

In the high Rockies of western Wyoming the land is rich under the dazzling sky of blue. The snow stays on the highest peaks all through the summer months and furnishes a sparkle that can now and again make a man snowblind, even in August. Along the sides of the mountains, in the long green valleys, the cattle graze; the herds having been pushed up that high so that the beeves can fatten themselves. There is always game in the tall timber and meadows—deer, pronghorn antelope, elk, bear; and there is the ubiquitous coyote who many maintain is the smartest survivor of all, the most adaptable to the ways of man, the great exterminator.

The days and nights are always fresh, crisp as a minted coin. For John Slocum there was no place like it in the whole of the great West. This was why he kept coming back; it was like coming home.

He knew the land like he knew his own hands. Now, a man with leather and steel in his bearing, honed by years of experience that included

horseflesh, cattle, and sheep, not only a knowledge of nature but of men, he was at home anywhere. For no matter where he went, he had himself. Some shrewd observers wondered if he could
be part Indian, so thoroughly had he learned his
craft, the craft of survival with man, beast, and
weather, so clearly did he have himself.

Now in his middle thirties, tall, lean, and broad-
shouldered, moving with the grace of a mountain
cat, he sat his high-canteled bronc saddle like he
was planted there. He always rode straight, yet
not at all stiff, easy, like an Indian, as though he
and his horse were one. It was striking, that grace
of movement in which even the slightest gesture
carried the whole man in it.

He had spent two days riding the country around
Hardtown, but mostly the range of which the DV
was a part, the range that included Dolly Dolores
and her girls as well as the other outfits: the Half
Circle Dot run by Jed Torgerson, Casper Flint's
Double-Back K, and Wendell Cole's Bar X.

As Slocum dismounted his pony and took out
his field glasses, he found himself wondering just
why Dolly Dolores was out here with her girls. The
conviction had been growing in him that she had to
be there for something extra. The money she'd be
making from her girls couldn't be all that much.

Sweeping the valley slowly with the glasses, he
had a long-distance look at all four spreads—
Torgerson's, Cole's, Flint's and Dolly's. And again
it struck him with even more force what an anomoly
Dolly was on that range. What was she *really* doing
there?

There was something missing. He saw this more

clearly as he wondered why anyone would want Dolly's DV Range. As far as he could tell there was nothing on that range that wasn't anywhere else. Was it that Torgerson and the others wanted to expand? Dolly had told him how Torgerson had offered a good price for the DV, but not all that good that she wanted to accept. That had been over a year ago, and Torgerson had never repeated his offer.

Then who was it sending the pair of bully-boys to set fire to the DV? Obviously, it was an attempt to scare Dolly off. Of course, by now the news was all around Hardtown; that somebody had tried to fire the DV.

He mounted the Appaloosa again and picked his way down one of the steeper trails high above the sweeping range. Slocum let his thoughts play over the situation. All the action since the first shot from Dolly Dolores's Henry rifle moved through his inner vision like a play, a story. Even the people he didn't know and hadn't met, such as Casper Flint, Wendell Cole, and Dolly's girls had their moment in his inner view as he tried to make sense out of what seemed more and more to be a snarled ball of wool.

It was plain that Dolly Dolores was bringing a needed service into the country—one that would be appreciated. Instead of having the girls in cribs in town, she had brought them out to where the customers lived and worked. Now, who could object to that? Some religious figure—a minister, a preacher, and surely some of the more prudish women. But those kinds of people wouldn't necessarily turn to violence.

And it was only then, as his thoughts led him through all the action that he had witnessed, that he now all at once realized what he had been actually, physically looking at. Plain as the proverbial pikestaff, he now saw the old man and the burro with the pack on its back, wending their way along the trail that led far below to the wooden bridge that spanned the narrow crossing of the Sawbuck River.

He saw the bridge quite clearly, even more so as he refocused his field glasses, taking in the logs and the crossed timbers and lumber planking that stretched over the triangular rock-and-log pilings that supported the span and around which the river now swirled.

All that detail sprang to his eye, into his mind, bringing with it thoughts on how the spring snows were melting high in the mountains and were rushing down through the valley, swelling the Sawbuck and even running over its banks here and there, while it rushed past Hardtown towards the south.

Now it was clear as the sun on the back of his hand. The two wooden handles sticking up from the pack on the burro's back, swinging back and forth as the animal picked his way carefully over the bridge, urged by the old man. Those two sticks could only be the handles of a pick and a shovel.

John Slocum reached into his shirt pocket and took out his makings and built himself a smoke. He sat there long enough to finish his cigarette, field strip it, and place the leavings in his shirt pocket. He was remembering something he had seen just outside Hardtown's general store only yesterday.

The mule team had been standing there, silent and passive in their shafts, as two men unloaded supplies that were then carried into the store. There had been the usual sacks of grain, barrels of nails, several boxes of the kinds of supplies that would be needed in any town in the ranch country—hammers, fence tools, wire, staples, manila rope. And, plain as the daylight that was covering the entire life of the town, shovels. A lot of them. He had caught them in a glance as he'd ridden by. Finally, a reason why the pressure was being put on Dolly Dolores's DV spread.

He struck the wooden lucifer one-handed with his thumbnail, canting his head toward the flame as he took his first puff, then he was up on his feet, his eyes squinting in the direction of the DV. Looking back at the bridge, he watched the old sourdough and his pack mule disappearing into the stand of willows on the far side of the Sawbuck.

It was then that he felt the man behind him, at the very moment that he saw the man in front of him stepping out of the stand of spruce trees. He had not been unaware of them, had heard them approaching but had wanted the confrontation. Especially now that he saw one good reason for the trouble Dolly Dolores was having.

"You're trespassin'," the taller of the two said, with his hand not far from the sixgun at his hip.

"Sorry," Slocum replied. "I didn't catch any sign sayin' this here was private property."

"Now you know," said the second man, almost a head shorter than his companion.

"Good enough."

They were both facing him now, hard, leaning into their words, eager for a move on his part. He knew the type. As a rule, they traveled in pairs, looking for trouble and finding it. Slocum was way ahead of them.

"Sorry, gents," he said softly, holding out his hands in a casual "search me" gesture.

In the next instant, he stepped forward and slapped the bigger man across his face, ducked, and kicked the second in his kneecap.

The recipient of that hard toe of his boot let out a scream of pain and surprise, while his companion swept his handgun from its holster.

"Drop it!" John Slocum's words were as hard as the barrel of the Colt .44 he was holding on the smaller man.

The gun that was only halfway out of its holster fell back into leather. Its owner's face was white, as empty of blood as his heart was now empty of courage.

"You're skinning it, mister!"

Slocum nodded. "That's right. I am skinning it." He looked at the man he had kicked in the kneecap. He had fallen to the ground, his face twisted in pain.

Swiftly, Slocum stepped over and relieved him of his sixgun. "Now then. We will start over. What is it you boys were saying?"

"This here is Half Circle Dot range, mister."

"That Torgerson?"

"It is. And Mister Torgerson don't take kindly to anyone trespassin'."

"Bully for him. Excepting this here is govern-

ment range. You better tell yer boss that. All this
land here is government." Swiftly, he holstered the
sixgun. His grin was cold as he looked down at the
man trying to get to his feet.

"You bust my leg!" He was a short, stocky man,
and his face was gray with pain, though there
were also flashes of red anger showing through
the gray.

"You should know better than to try a dumb
play like that," Slocum said. "You two got to be
green."

"There'll come a time, mister," said the man who
was up now, but clutching his knee, his face still
twisted in pain.

Slocum asked, "Where are your horses?" Then he
caught the sound in the stand of trees behind them
at the same time that he saw the man in front of
him throw a glance.

In that infinitesimal instant of hesitation Slocum
dove to his left side, away from the man in the trees,
and in the same split second, shot his would-be
drygulcher right through the throat.

"Get on your horses," he said, hard. "We're headin'
into Hardtown."

"Sheriff ain't gonna believe a word you tell him,
Slocum." It was the taller of the two saying it, and
his eyes flew to the man who had just been shot
and killed at the edge of the cottonwoods.

"Sorry to disappoint you boys," Slocum said.
"Only it ain't the sheriff we're going to pay a visit
to. It'll be somebody you'll be glad to see—one way
or the other."

"Who?" asked the man who had first tried to
throw down on Slocum.

"We'll be talking to Mister Bart Gooden, I reckon." And Slocum stepped swiftly up and onto the Appaloosa, not letting his eyes lose either one of his captives. "Now you two can ride double, but first you'll tie him onto the sorrel there, and you'll be leading him. Now move it. We don't have all night to get where we're going."

It didn't take long to get the body tied across the now empty saddle and another moment or two to pull out.

Slocum let them lead the way while he directed.

"We'll go visit Mister Gooden," he said again. "But first we're stopping by the DV."

"Gonna treat us to some sport, are you, Slocum?" said the bigger of the two. There was no smile on his face, but a sour downturn to his mouth. He was a clean-shaven man named Mick, and he was hairy, except for his face. He looked to Slocum as though he had some kind of skin disease, for his face was peeling. Then it crossed his mind that it could be unaccustomed to sunlight, supposing that he had worn a beard and had recently shaved. Why would a man suddenly decide to shave off his beard?

"Tell me your names," he said as they drew rein at a creek so that the horses could drink.

"Quince," said the clean-shaven man.

"My name's Billman," said his companion, his eyes narrowing as he looked at his captor. "And you, I seen you, Slocum, one time in Lander. Seen what you done to that feller tried to sass you. Seen the way you . . ."

"Shut it!" Slocum snapped. "Both of you shut it and ride. You're heading along the trail to the right there, and then when we cross the crick you'll go north."

"The DV, then Prairie Dog," said Quince. "Get yer fun, Slocum, 'fore Gooden and the boys make coyote shit outta you."

He didn't have time to regret those words; John Slocum and the Appaloosa were beside him quicker than a man could spit downwind. Billman's shocked "Holy Jees-us!" was lost as Quince was yanked out of his saddle and spilled onto the trail almost under the horses' hooves.

"Get back on the horse," Slocum said. "And keep your mouth shut. Next time, if you're stupid enough to try something again, next time you won't be able to ride him."

Dolly Dolores VanDam stood in the open doorway of her cabin and stared at the old man and his burro. She had said nothing upon opening the door to confront the visitor, nor had the old man. He must have been in his late sixties, maybe even seventy. Clearly, he'd been through his life. Gnarled, bent, with big horny hands like grab hooks, a grizzled face with long guttered cheeks ending in the bristle of a beard that looked too old and tired to go on growing. His hat looked to be as old as he was, and he wore only one suspender, which ran diagonally across his body. His trousers sagged, the crotch looking to the woman in the doorway as though he was carrying a load of tools within.

"Jesus," Dolly Dolores muttered. "Didn't figger ever to see hide nor hair of yeh in this good while. Christ Almighty!"

"The ways of the Lord," intoned the old sourdough standing before her, and he reached up and touched the chewed out brim of his Stetson with two fingers.

"Banyan Baldock is still alive an' kickin', as you can see, milady!" And his face opened like a broken walnut to emit a cackling.

Whatever he wanted, well, by Jesus, he'd damn well pay for it! Through that busted snout of his! Dolly knew him, she knew the old bugger from way back. She remembered, and by damn she'd never forget, that caper in Miller Butte. By damn! What the hell was going on here! First she heard old Elihu Lincoln Thong was in the country—just the other day Clyde Hollinger had said it—and now this. The old sonofabitch himself had to show up right on her doorstep! Somethin' goin' on here, and that was a gut!

"Good to see ya, Doll!"

"Well it sure ain't good to see you, you old buzzard! What you doin' here? I heard you was in Laramie."

"Laramie!" The explosion from that aged mouth with the dry, cracked lips caused the burro to take a step forward and break wind. "Gertrude, stop interruptin' now! Mind!" He turned back to Dolly. "Gonna ast me in, are you?"

"Come, you old buzzard. I want to hear what you be up to. What you doin' in this part of the country?" Suddenly she raised her head, looking, listening. "Anybody on your backtrail? Huh?"

"Man's got to get up pret-ty early in the mornin' to jigger old Banyan Baldock, by God! Huh! Hunh!" He shuffled forward, passing the halter rope over the hitching rail. "You wait here, Gertrude. Mind now!"

Scratching deep under one armpit he shuffled toward the door of the cabin where Dolly Dolores was waiting impatiently, her hard eyes checking the old boy's backtrail.

"You kin come in an' set. But mind, I got my sister with me, and you mind what you says." Her words sprayed the room as she entered and glared at the pot on the stove.

"Could use some arbuckle, and if you got any sourdough biscuits I'd be mighty appreciatin' for 'em." He opened his mouth then, revealing a wide gap where there were no teeth, and cackled mightily.

"Sound like a cock sizin' up how many he's figurin' to take on, by golly," said Dolly.

"I still rides the girls, by God I do!" And he shook with happy laughter so hard he began to cry and cough at the same time and collapsed into a chair that fortunately was handy to his rear end or he would have simply landed on the floor.

"Jesus . . ." muttered Dolly Dolores as the door opened and Sally walked in.

"I thought you must have company," the girl said. Looking at Banyan Baldock she smiled and held out her hand. "I'm Sally McQuarie, Dolly's sister."

The old man nodded, taking the proffered hand shyly, but then swiftly returning to his habitual role, he relaxed into a broad smile and winked hugely at Dolly.

"You sonofabitch! That is my kid sister you be

thinkin' about, and you cut that out or I'll cut yer balls off! I mean right now!" And she grabbed a butcher knife from the table that ran alongside the log wall next to the range.

"Dolly!" Sally stared in horror at her sister who was standing just to one side of her like a warrior ready for the kill.

"You sonofabitch, you keep your dirty hands and mouth and you know what else offa my sister. She is not the kind *you're* used to!"

"Calm yerself, Doll! Calm yerself! I come here to talk—uh—bizness." And he cocked his eye engagingly at her.

"The girls are down in the third cabin. Take yerself to the horse corral, then head toward the butte. It's a couple hundred feet, give or take. And there is three to choose from. However, I want to see the color of your money 'fore we go one step further!"

But the old boy was shaking his head. "Surprise ya, Doll; but I didn't come here for that. I got some business to talk over with you. Private like." And he tossed an engaging glance at Sally.

"I have got some sewing to attend to in the bedroom," Sally said, picking up on it, and she turned on her heel.

"Good enough," Dolly Dolores said. Crossing the room she reached into a basket by the horsehair sofa and drew out a bottle.

"By cracky, that is more like it!" And old Banyan Baldock was covered with smiles, his forehead slightly damp from the exertion of trying to follow the social amenities, while at the same time sticking to what was becoming more and more obvious as urgent business.

When Sally had left the kitchen, Dolly lifted her glass. "So?"

"So," said Banyan Baldock and addressed himself to the brown fluid, raising his glass, smiling, and then downing.

"Prime," he said as though tasting the word. "Prime. I do favor it. And thank God you got the good hospitality to serve real liquor and not that trail piss what they got in them saloons all over the goddamn frontier!" And his cackle rattled over the log walls as he scratched under each arm and sniffed mightily.

Meanwhile, Dolly Dolores was watching him with her malevolent eyes at half mast, but the old boy didn't appear to mind. He'd been around a long time and aplenty.

"Get to the action, you old buzzard. Who sent you, and what does he want?"

Banyan Baldock was already chuckling, sniffing, reaching back to his rear teeth with his tongue to extract a piece of wild venison that had been stuck there since breakfast and no matter what he tried he couldn't get it loose.

"Ten'll get you twenty you know him already," Banyan said.

"Name wouldn't begin with a . . ."

"Never mind!" snapped Banyan, cutting her off. "I was tolt never to mention no names, and I figger you ought to of bin the same. So watch yer talkin' there." And he felt good for the first time since he'd run into her again, good that he'd taken charge of the conversation. Of course, it didn't last. But while it was there he enjoyed it.

"This party," he said slowly, and then paused to take a long pull at his drink. "This party, the same what set you up in this here . . ." And he spread his hands. "By the way, how many girls you got in there?" And he threw his head in the direction of the girls' cabin.

"Got three. But can always use another." Dolly Dolores pursed her lips and studied her companion with hard eyes, as though he was a total stranger. Yet, she'd known him, had worked with him in K.C. Singleton, Terry River, and Dodge.

"The—uh—feller. Himself there. He is working on somethin' what kin make us all a whole helluva lot of do-re-mi."

"I am not against that," Dolly Dolores said firmly. "Just tell me what he has told you to tell me and fer Chrissake let's cut the palaver. Get down to the action, will you." She reached out and swept his glass from right under his reaching hand.

But old Banyan Baldock was no amateur. His own hand dove to the rescue, grabbing the glass, while his other hand locked firmly around her wrist. And for a moment they struggled, with the result that the half-filled glass of whiskey fell to the floor and broke, glass and fluid flying in every direction.

"Shit!"

"I'll favor another drink, Madame VanDam!" He was standing now and facing her from every inch of his attention. He was furious.

"Get to the point, you old buzzard," snapped Dolly. "I ain't used to getting news from himself through some hired hand, fer Chrissakes!"

"Bullshit! Bullshit! Bullshit! You listen to me! Hear?" He started toward the door as though leaving, but then stopped and returned to his chair. In a calmer voice he said, "Look, let's get on with it. We both got to handle it like it comes. So leave us cut the bull and get to handling things like the easiest."

She stood glaring at him at length as he remained silent, then she appeared to soften. "Y'old buzzard. Always did want to get yer own way, didn't ya!"

He cocked his eye at her then as she handed him a fresh glass of booze. "Always wanted to get into yer pants, that's what I wanted, my gal." And he chuckled and chortled and began scratching himself on the backs of his arms, in his crotch, and along the back of his neck.

"It'll be a cold day in the middle of July when that happens, you old bugger."

"I happen to be one of them fellers—and seems like you cotton to that type, my girl—what sticks to his guns. Man like me sets his cap for a filly, he don't allow hisself to get put off the track. But . . ." And he held up his hand, palm facing her, and it flashed through her mind how smooth it was. "First, let's get down to business. I bin talkin' to himself and also to a feller name of Lincoln."

"Lincoln!" Her hand flew to her mouth. "But he's—"

"Not Abe. Fer Chrissakes, you think I'm cuckoo! I am talking about that lawyer or judge feller or whatever the hell he calls hisself. Thong. Lincoln Thong or Thong Lincoln."

"Elihu Lincoln Thong," said Dolly Dolores. "Hmmm . . ."

"You know the feller!"

"Not carnally."

"Not who?"

"Not in the flesh."

"You mean, you ain't screwed him."

"That's it exactly."

"Interestin'."

"Interesting! What the hell d'you mean, interesting? What's so damn interesting!"

"The fact you ain't screwed him. Mebbe one of your girls done so."

"No."

"What d'you mean No? Maybe you don't know everythin' what goes on, even though you thinks you do."

She drew herself up to her full angry height at that and said, "Mister, I know plenty."

"Do you know who's about to discover a gold mine about as far from here as you can spit in a high wind then?"

And with that delivered right between the ribs, old Banyan Baldock sniffed, reached for his drink, and at the same time drew a cigar from his shirt pocket. He was, he told himself, feeling just like a million dollars.

They hadn't been riding more than a couple of hours before Slocum picked up the trail of the old-timer with the burro. Pure chance, plus the fact that they'd had to cross the Sawbuck and had done so over the very same bridge where Slocum had seen the old prospector and his burro, plus the pick and shovel. And it was just as they reached the other side of the river that he made up his mind as to what he was going to do.

It was clear now that the old man was heading in the direction of the DV. It was clear too that he wasn't going to be getting much out of the pair of hooligans who were clearly working for Gooden.

"I'm letting you go," he said, drawing rein. "And you can tell Gooden I'll be up to see him when I've attended to some other business."

They said nothing. They sat their ponies looking at him. Neither the pair of them nor the dead man said a word.

"Now git," Slocum said. "You tell Gooden to keep himself and his boys off DV Range."

He sat the Appaloosa, watching them out of sight. Well, the message was out now. There would be no more fencing. He could feel the lines being drawn; indeed he had done just that by declaring war on Bart Gooden.

It would have been good to follow up on Gooden's men, but the prospector was the more important aspect to pursue. What was an old prospector doing on range where there was about as much chance of gold being found as there was of palm trees growing in the bottom of the ocean?

Well, he'd not known the likes of Sally McQuarie since he could remember, and now that good-looking girl with the charming smile, soft voice, and delightful eyes and body was within a half-hour ride. The old prospector had given him an extra reason for going to see that young lady instead of looking up the likes of Bart Gooden.

Now, feeling the sun strong on the backs of his

hands, he kicked the Appaloosa into a brisk canter, riding easy, fully alert to what he had known even before the trio had braced him—that the whole play of the three men had been a feint. Gooden had no business with him, nor had he any real reason for causing trouble at the DV.

No, there was something else at hand, something much bigger than highway robbery, stagecoach looting, or even train hold-ups or the rivalry over graze. He was by no means sure what it was, but he could smell it. It was big, and it was right here and now.

As he rode, he tried to keep the girl at the back of his mind. He was not the man to bust everything over a beautiful girl, and he wasn't the sort to lose his head over other parts of his or anyone else's anatomy either.

8

The room was thick with cigar smoke, the odor of booze, the hum-and-hive of men talking, laughing, exchanging conviviality, although each was on guard, aware of how he must behave, guarding against the wrong word, facial expression, or give-away gesture.

There were a dozen of these gentlemen, and they filled the spacious private room at the Cheyenne Club in Lannerton. These were the stockgrowers, the Association, the men who had "built the West," and were still building it.

Torgerson was there, and so was Casper Flint, and Wendell Cole from the Hardtown country. There were other big men from the Lander and Buffalo ranges, men who had weathered the Big Freeze, the terrible winter of the Great Die-Up when the whole of the West had turned to ice, and the stockmen had faced ruin. No one had come through that terrible time unscathed, and no one would ever forget it, how it was, how it must never happen again.

But it wasn't going to be easy. The government wasn't much help. Of course the stockmen had their men in Washington, their spokesmen, their agents, but there wasn't all that much a man could do. And it was wise to cover your bets, and then cover your covers. A man had to play it but damn close.

"A man needs a man in Washington," was how Royal Thor Undershaft had put it. Undershaft knew how to handle a word. That was for sure.

At the present meeting, as they finished off the luncheon with brandy and cigars, with for most of them a look forward to some fun with the girls later on (all at Roy Undershaft's expense) they took in the gist if not the meat and potatoes of Undershaft's talk.

"What you men, what *we*, need in the north-western section of the Wyoming Territory, gentlemen, is a railroad." The statement, bald as the head of the American eagle, fell onto the table with the finality of aces. "You—excuse me again, gents, *we*—" Accompanied by a little laugh, "We need to band together to do everything we can to have our representatives in the U.S. government do as we wish; that is to say, since we are the ones who back them, then by the Lord Harry we need to see to it that our reps are informed. Not only that . . ." He held up a hand to stifle the applause, always a little premature when booze had been served. "Not only that, we must damn well see to it that our needs are taken care of!"

Applause, followed by more applause.

"But how? We need a plan, it seems to me." This from a big rancher from the Blue River country, named Thomason. "All very well to know what we want, all very well to lay our money for to see that our interests are not overlooked, but where's the guarantee?"

Undershaft was smiling, having planted the question in Thomason's head just a little while earlier, before they had sat down to lunch; he was waiting for it.

"I am indeed glad that you asked that question, sir! Shows a man is thinking, as the saying goes." He paused, while someone started to clap; someone else said, "Hear-hear!" And there was general goodwill sweeping around the table. The dozen men were coming together, just the way Roy Undershaft wanted it! Just the way he had planned it!

"Gentlemen! What is the difference between our situation in the northern country, say around Hardtown and the Blue River country, and let us say, the Comstock Lode?"

There followed an immediate, stunned silence at these words. Undershaft was smiling. The smile turned into a grin as the silence lengthened. Everyone was stymied by mention of the Comstock.

"Can't see what the comparison could possibly be," said a man named Harrels. He had streaks of gray in his thick head of hair, though his hairline was receding, and he was obviously approaching his older years. Yet a vigorous man, Edward Harrels had been through it—not as a cattleman but as banker. He had been at the core of the old days when the Great Die-Up had savaged the whole of the Western cattle market.

Harrels had been sitting back in his chair, but

now he leaned forward with his elbows on the big table around which the dozen men were gathered, with his fingers making an arch as the ten tips touched each other.

Undershaft almost split his face in a grin. He'd been waiting for just such a remark. Sober as an undertaker at his own funeral, he dealt his fistful of aces.

"The comparison is quite possible, I'd say. I'd hazard the guess that it would be quite possible, for Hardtown to emulate—yes, emulate— the Comstock story. *If . . .*" and he held high a forefinger, pausing for them to take in that powerful two-letter word, "*if* the conditions were similar. The same!"

"You're saying that if there was a strike in Hardtown, if someone discovered gold or silver that . . ."

But this was premature to Undershaft's plan, and he cut the man off. Jed Torgerson it was, a man who took and said and did everything literally.

Undershaft, smooth as a newly greased axle slipped in with, "Ah yes, the Comstock. You gentlemen were there. Or some of you must have been. I am in no position to tell you men what it was like! Even though I was there. I am sure some of you were, too," he went on, with emphasis, knowing very well that only one or two had actually been on the Comstock at its height, all being busy at home with their cattle.

His gambit worked. They were listening. "Let me tell you how it was from the eye of an amateur, a visitor, and yet a man who knows about gold and silver strikes—myself. I have been to several strikes, not only the Comstock, but Tombstone, Leadville, and maybe all of the big ones." He paused, letting it sink in, letting it be accepted that he, himself, was an expert. Modest, to be sure, but one who could impart inside information about certain key situations.

"Need I remind you gentlemen how the discovery of silver changed the face of the entire West—nay, even the face of the United States?" He paused.

Then Big Bill Brennan bit. "Are you suggesting that there might be, or maybe even is such a possibility in the Hardtown and Prairie Dog country? Gold?" His careful glance swept the table. "May I say the word 'gold'?"

There was a tense pause. Feet were shuffled. Hands reached for glasses.

"Or, what about the possibility—I say possibility—of silver?" Undershaft's soft voice moved into the atmosphere as though somebody had opened a window.

"You did mention the Comstock?" somebody brought the word in from, it seemed, nowhere.

"I did." Undershaft inclined his large head, very gently as though in church. After all, as Jed Torgerson was thinking, the subject of a silver strike in Hardtown of all places and the Sawbuck River country did call for a tone of reverence.

A distinguished silence had indeed fallen on the group, and at that moment Undershaft signaled the waiter who was standing in a corner of the room to serve more drinks.

The ritual was conducted in silence. At its conclusion, the host signaled the waiter to leave the room.

"Gentlemen . . ." Royal Undershaft leaned slightly forward with the fingers of both hands laced together on the table in front of him. "Gentlemen, I of course am not, I repeat *not*, in any way suggesting that there is even the possibility of a gold or silver strike in the northern Wyoming Territory. It is, well, it seems, impossible; let me put it that way. It's just that for some reason or other the activity, the excitement, the new life that poured into the Comstock comes to mind. Why, I mean to say, the whole life of the country was transformed overnight. I mean, I was there!" He paused, his fingers touching his chin.

"But you know," he went on, "you know how those years in Virginia City were utterly fantastic. The farther into the earth the mines went, the wider became the silver vein and the richer its contents. Gentlemen, as you likely know, the Comstock Lode was found to continue clear across Mount Davidson and well beyond on both sides. Why, exploration shafts went down 2,000 feet with no end to the ore in sight. Crosscuts showed the vein to be from 50 to 200 feet wide, ending in walls of barren porphyry. Then—mind you!—somebody guessed that the porphyry might not be the main body of rock that produced the Sierra Nevada mountains, so the cuts were extended for a few feet, and new veins of ore, running as high as $1,000 a ton, were discovered!"

"Incredible," someone muttered. And around the table heads were shaking, eyes were staring into space, awe had descended, as indeed it always did when the Comstock was mentioned.

Roy Undershaft watched the proceedings coolly, letting his words stay where they were in the atmosphere, working slowly but firmly on the group gathered at the table. He had once told his lady acquaintance how he worked hard to create atmosphere. "You see, it is atmosphere that affects people a whole lot more than facts and figures. And the value, my dear, is that it goes unnoticed as such. One is on guard against facts and figures, but atmosphere knows no barriers. There is no way of protecting oneself from atmosphere, unless—of course," he added, "one already knows about it and is therefore prepared."

He remembered this part of the conversation, but the rest had vanished. Even now it was gone as he sat at the table in the Cheyenne Club pumping his pitch to the gang of cattlemen and bankers. By God, it was hard sometimes to keep his mind off the luscious body that had pleasured him with such frequency over the past year and a half. The only difficulty being that that delightful person wanted to marry him.

"But you gentlemen must realize," he heard himself saying now, even before the sense of it came into his thought, "what could happen to a town such as Hardtown if such a happy calamity occurred."

"About as much chance as a cat having dog pups," said Torgerson with a sarcastic sneer. Undershaft felt like letting him have it.

"Nobody is saying it will happen to Hardtown, even though the Northern Pacific is interested in a depot and possibly even a cattle shipping point there."

"Be all right with me," said Wendell Cole. "Bring some life to the town."

"And money," somebody put in.

"The point is," cut in Undershaft, "there isn't a prayer the Northern Pacific will even look at the place. I've made a thorough investigation of the possibilities."

A man with long, gray hair who was known all over the northern country as Hairy River Bill snorted. His actual name was Carl Parton, and he owned a good bit of beef up on the north fork of the Sawbuck. He snorted again and said, "Hell's bells, somethin's got to be done or that damn town is going to just dry up and blow away. And there ain't a man at this table don't know it. Now, God dammit, we all of us went to some trouble to haul ass down here and palaver with Undershaft. Dammit to hell, let's get to somethin' more than just beatin' our gums!"

"I second that!" said a thin man with buck teeth, one of which was missing, leaving a pretty wide gap. "I second that," he said again. "We got to do somethin' 'bout makin' Hardtown a community. Hell, I says, if Virginia City coulda done it, then why not us. I don't mean we got to go the whole hog. But we got to do somethin'."

"Like strike it rich, huh!" snorted a potbellied man named Carlson. He was potbellied, yes, and this facet of his physique had caused some persons throughout Carlson's life to make the vast mistake of assuming that he was frail or inept because of his huge belly. They'd found out that they had not only been wrong, but disastrously wrong.

For a few more moments, Undershaft allowed the conversation to chew back and forth on what he had thrown at the table; that is, the pros and cons of the future of Hardtown. Then he decided it had gone far enough. The group was at the point where he wanted them.

"Seems to me we need some kind of miracle," he said softly, but there wasn't a man at the table who didn't hear those words.

"You got one?" Casper Flint asked.

At that point Undershaft snapped his fingers, and the waiter who had been standing at the door came forward and handed him a white piece of paper. That is to say, the waiter brought the sheet of paper to the table and leaned forward to place the paper on the table in front of Undershaft.

"I have here a statement which you may all read; in fact, I shall ask Rogers here, my personal valet, to read it to you in a moment. It simply states that I am to be put in charge of all operations necessary to the purpose we will now outline and which will deal with the revitalization of Hardtown and its environs."

"Just what are you getting at? That's what I'd like to know, Undershaft." It was Torgerson speaking.

Undershaft smiled at him, though not with a great deal of warmth. "The paper will tell you the details of the discovery of gold on North Buffalo Range and will be in effect a contract with myself and my company to assign rights to whoever wishes to either mine or simply own a section of range land—and do with it what they like."

If he had fired a round of bullets in the room, the company couldn't have been more shocked.

When the astonishment finally began to subside, Undershaft looked at each face coolly, then he said, "Well, gentlemen, is there any one of you who does not wish to sign?"

"I would just like to know how you figger there is gold there," Torgerson said.

"Yes," chipped in a man named Bailey. "How come you know there's gold there and nobody else 'pears to?"

Roy Undershaft smiled a very wide smile at that question. Later, in bed with his paramour, he was asked just that same question.

"Darling, how do you know there's gold there?"

He had smiled at her. "I don't know."

"But what did you tell the people at the luncheon then?"

"Same thing. I didn't know."

She snuggled closer to him. "And what did they say to that?"

He had chuckled. "They just looked at me, and I told them simply that I was sure there would be when the moment came for it to be necessary."

And he had rolled over on top of her then. "Now let's handle some much more serious material," he said as he squeezed a breast, and brought his knee up between her legs.

But he couldn't resist adding, "You see, my dear, it was their greed told them there was gold there. Not Royal Thor Undershaft."

To his great joy, he found that she was alone in the cabin; Dolly Dolores had ridden off to check something or other with a visitor.

"She left with an old man named Banyan Baldock." Sally told him. "Said they were going to take a look at something up near Pitchfork Creek."

"How far is that?" he asked, taking his hat off as she stepped back to let him in.

"I don't know. I don't know this country very well. But I think it isn't far."

"And they just took off like that?"

She nodded. They were silent for a moment while she brought coffee and some biscuits from the stove.

"You came at exactly the right moment," she said, and he caught the fleeting smile in her face.

"In time for the biscuits, or for your worry?" he asked, looking gently at her.

"You're a very sensitive man, Mister Slocum."

"Yes, maybe. And you're a very sensitive young woman, Miss McQuarie."

They both laughed then.

"I mean Sally," he said.

"Yes—er—John. Isn't your name John, sir?"

"It has been, but if you don't like it I can easily change it," he said.

Her laughter tinkled all over him as their eyes met. "That'll be the day, when you change anything of yourself for anybody," she said.

"I don't consider you anybody."

"I do not consider you, sir, as anybody either. So there!"

And they were laughing together.

A moment of silence fell then, and at last he said, "Tell me what you're worried about."

"It's about Dolly. She hasn't been the same since that person, that man, came by here and spent quite a while with her."

"What man? Baldock?"

"No, that one named Bart Gooden. Doll sent me out of the room, so I don't know what they talked about, only that she was really shaken after he left."

"Shaken?"

"Angry, and I could see that she was worried as well. That man, he's evil. I had a good look at him, and I am not happy about Dolly getting mixed up with such a person."

"Tough was he?"

She looked down at her hands lying in her lap. "I don't know what he was. He seemed all right. I mean his behavior, how he was, the way he talked to her, all that was fine. There was just something else, something I couldn't make out."

"Something mysterious?" Slocum asked, trying to draw it out. "Secretive?"

"That was it—he was secretive. I mean, it was quite plain that he didn't want me around, even though he wasn't saying anything special, only sort of hinting at, well, like where he'd been and where he was going, and then something about mister somebody-or-other. I didn't catch the name."

"But how was your sister with all this? Was it mysterious to her, do you think?"

"Well, yes and no. At first she didn't seem to get what he was talking about, something about the lay of the land and what surprises you could find."

"And he'd found something?"

"Well, you see, he never actually said so. He didn't say anything definite. And he kept looking at her as though she ought to know what he was talking about, what he was hinting at."

"Hunh . . ."

"What's that?"

"I said 'Hunh'."

"Hmm, I believe is more appropriate," she said. "If I might allow a little brightness into the gloom that seems to have covered us." She smiled at him with delight. "Eh?"

"No . . ." He shook his head. " 'Hunh' is more appropriate than 'Hmm'." He nodded, agreeing with what he had just said, his face dead serious. "Yes, I think we've got it settled now."

"Settled? On Hmm?"

"No. On Hunh."

By now they were both shaking with laughter, and in the next moment he had his arms around her.

"There's only one way to settle this argument," he said.

"I should say 'settle this dispute'," she insisted, but her lips found his before he could reply.

And that was the end of it.

And the beginning of the removal of clothes, the locking of her bedroom door—that is, barricading it, for the door had no lock and key.

He mounted her eagerly, and she received him in the same marvelously happy vein; her legs clutching him to her, her arms circling his neck, while he had her buttocks in both his hands as she pumped to receive his organ deeper and deeper with each already soaking stroke. Until they both exploded in the exquisite ultimate joy, dissolving in a deliciously soft tangle of arms and legs and little whimpers which finally turned into sighs of happiness.

At The Best Time Saloon the action was brisk. As always, except in the very early hours of first daylight, the barroom was crowded. With three or four deep at the long mahogany bar, the two bartenders were getting as much sweat as booze into the whiskey they were pouring. The faro players were so crowded the dealer had to keep warning the onlookers to move back. The poker tables and the dice game were even worse. Even the two wheels of fortune were hemmed in by the crowd.

Jammed into a corner of the room, Banyan Baldock and his companion sat close enough to rub knees.

"You keep yer paw offa my leg, you big hunk of mutton," snarled Dolly Dolores.

"Accident, my dear. My apologies. Just reachin' fer my money to buy us another round." He beamed at her, closing his right eye, apparently in a wink.

Watching him, Dolly Dolores winced. "Bet y'ain't had a bath in a month. You smell like a Rocky Mountain goat, for Chrissakes!"

"Remember the last time, don't ya?" he said, beaming.

"I'd just as soon fergit it. Drunk as a piss-ant you were. Couldn't stand up. Fallin' all over the place . . ."

"But it was a good time had, eh?" And he cackled and slapped his thigh, reaching over to pinch her bare arm.

Her reaction was instantaneous, and he reeled from the blow, almost falling out of his chair. Yet it wasn't the force of her punch that sent him reeling, but his own laughter which bubbled up like a geyser, and now he sat holding the edge of the table, tears streaming from his old eyes, roaring, coughing, sniffling with the hilarity of the moment.

His companion regarded him with her most pungent loathing, though at the same time she was not unaware that some of the onlookers were regarding her with fresh eyes. What the hell, sure she was no spring chicken, but she wasn't some rigid old fowl neither!

He signalled for another round, but the bartender paid no attention, so now he rose and walked carefully to the bar, carefully secured a bottle and came back to the table.

She had watched all this more or less with one eye, while with the other she was checking the population and their worth, always in the light of her present career. But at the same time she was wondering what the old buzzard wanted. Sure he wanted to get it—who didn't, for Chrissake? But he clearly was after something else. He had a message to deliver, which he was doing in between grabbing a leg here and there, the old bugger. She knew him well, a long time, in and out of bed.

She trusted him as far as she could lift a team of horses, but she knew too that he was a connection with whoever was trying to take over the valley, the town, the northern range. She'd a notion who it was, but wouldn't bet on a name. Wouldn't for the matter of that, even mention a name. She knew her onions if she knew anything. Had learned at an early age that two plus two equals four, but also that two and two make twenty-two, by God!

"It ain't the best place to talk, this here," she said, trying a new tack.

"It's the best. I was told to bring you here. It's the best just on account it's the one nobody expectin' to talk something serious like you an' me would figure on."

He was right. She had known this, but wanted to test him. He wasn't too bright, and she saw right off that it was going to have to be herself in charge. The delicacy was that you had to be real careful. One wrong move in handling another person and you'd find yerself up shit crick.

At the same time, she was mindful of the way old Banyan Baldock had opened their conversation, with reference to the gold being mined on the far side of Carter Mountain. How come? Sure, they were digging out gold, but not a helluva lot, and also that was on the other side; there wasn't even a flake of the yellow stuff around Hardtown. She was no expert in this kind of thing, but she was no dumbbell neither.

"I ain't blind, Banyan, you old buzzard. I can see you an' that animal walking all over the country here, but you ain't gonna find enough gold to physic a jaybird. I'd lay my last dollar on that."

He had listened to her, leaning heavily on the table, his lips pursed, his rheumy eyes alight with laughter and, to her vast irritation, an apparently superior knowledge. Leastways, that was the impression he was delivering.

He leaned even further forward now, and holding her with his creamy look, he said, "Thing is, my girl, I ain't lookin' for any gold. And neither is himself."

"Himself?"

"You know who I'm talkin' about."

"Do I?"

"If you don't then we both be wastin' time."

She started to speak, but his palm was suddenly only inches from her mouth. "No names. Fer Chrissake!"

"God dammit! I wasn't fixin' to say any name, you asshole! What the hell d'you think I am? And who the fuck d'you think you are, lecturin' me like that. Go fuck yerself!" And she rose from the table, a wall of fury, and strode through the crowd to the swinging doors and out, leaving that old man with his mouth hanging open, his eyes tearing with laughter.

9

The trail was dusty and forlorn with only the suspicion of game anywhere nearby. It was on the far side of Bitter Mountain, which rose like a finger straight north of the DV and neighboring outfits covering the high country above Hardtown. Slocum didn't need anybody to tell him this was the wildest and most inaccessible country in the Breeder Hills. This was where Prairie Dog was located. The narrow mountain trail gave out after close to an hour's riding, and Slocum was faced with only dense, almost impassable underbrush of scrub oak and blackjack.

After a short ride through the cluster that was all but impenetrable, he found himself on a dry creek bed that he figured would take him through the valley at the right side of the mountain, and—from rumor, partial information and pure guesswork— he hoped to reach Prairie Dog. But the going was slow, for the creek bed soon became a matted jungle of more scrub oak and blackjack. He found that he could barely move, so he dismounted and, with difficulty, led the horse.

After about an hour climbing almost vertically up a nearly invisible trail, he saw a clearing ahead and felt sure he was really close to Prairie Dog. As he stood at the edge of the small clearing he could see that the whole area was in fact a series of box canyons, and finding a new position, he discovered that he now had a good view of the box canyon directly below him.

This, however, made him even more cautious to be on the watch for outriders. He had seen two on his way into the maze of canyons, but knew that there had to be more. Gooden was a hard man and a careful one. He would surely have everything covered as far as security went.

Now, shifting his position he had a perfect view of what had to be Prairie Dog. He spotted a log hut or cabin across the small canyon on the side of a high cliff.

He saw too how the box canyon was of the type characteristic of the Rocky Mountains; that is, natural rock cliffs made walls on three sides and left a grassy floor with water in it. Thus it made a perfect corral when any sort of closure was maintained at the bottom end. He figured it was at least a mile long. There was a horse race in progress, and he counted nearly twenty men, give or take, for some kept moving out of view and others kept appearing. It was a good distance from where he was and difficult to register details.

But he didn't want to hang around. Gooden was no easy mark—Bart Gooden or Bart Rankin. He was pretty sure they were the same person. He had known Rankin back in Mojave—a mean, tough, backshooting slicker. Dangerous from the moment he set eyes on you. Rankin, Gooden—he had to be the same. There couldn't be two such men about. Slocum reflected on that grimly.

He remembered the story of Bart Rankin shooting an old man who had somehow displeased him. He had literally shot him to pieces. First one arm, then the other, then his legs, then his stomach, his chest, taking careful aim against his defenseless victim and making sure he didn't die too soon.

He had heard the story and had his doubts about it, thinking maybe it was partly true. But on meeting the man in the flesh, he knew right now that it had to be the truth. That Rankin-Gooden was a 14-carat sonofabitch, and there could be no argument about it.

They had crossed paths just the one time. The scene was the livery in a town called Bulow, on the border between Idaho and Wyoming. Slocum had been shoeing his horse, had spent more than a couple of hours at it, for she was a feisty sorrel mare with a temper to match the red. When he slipped slightly in some horse manure while holding her foreleg between his own legs in order to file her hoof, she'd jumped, pulled back, and snapped her halter.

It had taken him a minute to gentle her, which was no difficulty; he'd simply spoken to her. But suddenly there had been this angry voice behind him.

"Hoss ever pull that shit on me I'd sure as hell cut'm to size."

Slocum had held his tongue and had continued with his shoeing work. In a minute or two he heard a loud smack, and a big black horse came rearing back toward him. It was ridden by the owner of that hard, harsh voice.

Slocum had put down his clippers with which he'd been trimming the mare's hooves.

"Mister, I don't believe I care for you more than about a piece of nothing." His tone was as hard as the handle of the clippers he'd just dropped to the ground.

And in the next instant, the big, wide, burly man had swept his right hand toward a gun in his unbuttoned shirt.

Only to be staring into Slocum's Colt .44.

Slocum's next invitation had not been cordial. "Just drop it out on the ground there."

As the big man's belly gun hit the ground, Slocum holstered his Colt, stepped forward, and slapped him across his face, hard. He staggered.

Slocum holstered his own gun and waited. The two of them stood facing each other. Finally, it was the other who ended it. He spat on the ground, and said, "We'll meet again. The name is Bart Rankin. Don't forget it."

"I already have," Slocum had said. And he'd stood there, holding the other with his hard eyes until Rankin turned and without a word walked away.

Yes, he was thinking now as he looked down at the box canyon, Gooden was more than likely Rankin. Fate, circumstance, whatever you wanted to call it.

Now he saw the two men approaching. He'd spotted them, down by the horse racing, had seen the reflection of sunlight on field glasses. He could have gotten away, but the fact was he wanted to come in openly.

Now, as he looked into the barrels of the drawn guns, he grinned. "You boys can put those shooters away, I ain't going to draw on you."

"Mister Gooden is waiting to see you, Slocum. We had you ever since you come in at the other end of the canyon." The man was not trying to hold the triumph back from his words.

"That's what I know," Slocum said. "I been expecting you ever since one of you was dumb enough to light up your cigar back where I crossed that creek with the willows."

They looked sour at that.

"Listen Slocum, watch yer . . ."

But before he could say anything, Slocum slapped him across the face—backhanded.

"No, mister. You watch it!"

His companion started to move, but stopped as suddenly as he'd started, for Slocum's .44 was looking him in the face. Those two men from Prairie Dog froze in their boots, the color draining from their faces.

"We'll go visit Gooden, or Rankin, or whatever his name is," Slocum said, his voice easy, his movement swift and smooth as the sixgun returned to its holster. "You can lead the way."

"Tim, you go back of him," said the taller of the two, the one who had tried to brace Slocum.

"I want both of you in front of me," Slocum said, leaning real hard into his words.

10

Nobody could remember how it actually started. As an oldtimer pointed out, and it was a long time afterwards, it was kind of like the weather. Everything was calm, cool, collected, and then out of nowhere and without the least bit of warning *it* was there. *It* had driven men crazy, from Jim Marshall and his fabulous discovery, to the Comstock, to Tombstone. GOLD. The rumor alone, often without the least shred of actual support, drove men to Herculean deeds, both brave and knavish. Murder was nothing in comparison to the heat of passion that was engendered by even the whisper, even the thought of such a word.

Nor did it need actually to be spoken. It was in a shrug, a lifted eyebrow, a sniff. Like a trigger releasing a dam into a flood, releasing a power no one could stop, which would only settle once it had spent itself. And the point was, there never was expected to be any rhyme or reason for it. For that single word, mountains would be scaled, boiling rivers forded at floodtime, men slaughtered, and dreams savaged. Gold. That four-letter word that had driven men to insanity, to cruelty beyond description, though seldom if ever to nobility. As Elihu Lincoln Thong had only just pointed out to the small gathering at Prairie Dog.

It was the gathering to which Slocum had been escorted, and he now found himself in the presence of the man he had been expecting: Bart Gooden—Bart Rankin. Take your pick, as he said on meeting the big muscleman again.

"Anyway you favor it, Slocum, but far as you're concerned, the name is Gooden, and you remember it! You hear!"

Slocum didn't answer. He was looking around the room. The two men who had confronted him outdoors had left, and he was in what appeared to be the main cabin facing Gooden and three gunslingers who seemed to be bodyguards of a sort, though he knew that a man such as Gooden didn't need such extras. The man was tough, and he was fast. That had to be admitted, no matter how much you might dislike the sonofabitch.

Actually, Slocum was feeling pretty good about running into Elihu Lincoln Thong again. And while it was clear that Bart Gooden was the commanding presence of the gathering, Thong was a definite factor. Slocum saw right off that the old boy was no passive follower of Gooden. The half-dozen men who made up the remainder of the group obviously were members of the Prairie Dog group, the Gooden gang.

"So what is it you want, Slocum." Gooden stood hard in front of him, his arms at his sides, hands ready either to go for his brace of guns, or to raise his fists. "You be interrupting us, me and the boys, so I hope you got a good reason, and say it right now." His eyes had swept the group as he said those words, now resting on Elihu, thus placing him in the category of being one of his men.

This fine point was not missed by Slocum, who was delighted at Thong's reaction.

"You better ast me the same, Gooden, by Jesus. On account of I want it clear as daylight, and I mean right now, that I ain't no part, never was, and never wish to be of yore outfit, which far as I am concerned can go piss in a high wind for all you're worth. I—shut up!" he snapped as Gooden started to speak. "I ain't anywheres even begun to start to finish what I commenced to say! And that is, I am here independent on my ownsome with nothing owed to nobody, no thing, no place, or person, or group. I got myself, by God, and that is all I figger to need in this world. An' maybe any other for the matter of that."

The words came out of him in a torrent, and the gathering seemed to Slocum to gasp as they stared in astonishment. But none of this could derail the great barrister. And indeed, he swept on as though nothing had happened, as though he was solely in command of the group's attention, which, in point of fact, he was.

"Let us be happy that we have such a man as John Slocum visiting our fine community. We should feel blessed for the occasion, for the kindness of that which knows better, greater than we mortals."

He swept his hat from his unruly head of hair, his head dropped, and his chin hit his chest, as though his throat had been cut, and he plunged to the floor, landing on one knee with a thud, his face wincing in pain.

Nobody knew how to handle it. There was nowhere to look, no role to take. Slocum lowered his head slightly, just enough to keep in touch with Elihu's move, but not enough to commit himself in any opposition to the rest of the group. He saw that embarrassment had gripped the gathering, with Bart Gooden not knowing where to look. It was good seeing the sonofabitch uneasy, and he wanted to grin but withheld it.

Nor was Elihu at any loss as he got to his feet. "Mr. Gooden, I suggest you dismiss your men, and you and Slocum here and myself can talk." He was glaring with a most evident distaste at the big bully, but without the least drop of fear. Slocum could see that some of the men were at a loss at the turn of events.

A silence held the room now, and all could hear a pack rat scampering around one of the logs that formed the foundation of the cabin.

Suddenly, Gooden jerked his head, and the men began to file out. For a split second, Slocum's attention was on Elihu Thong who so surprisingly had taken over command of the action. In that second, a warning like a stab of lightning cut through him, and he moved just in time to catch the fist that Gooden had thrown at him like a cannonball. It was as hard too, as though it had indeed been fired from a cannon, and he almost fell as it landed on the side of his head, at the temple, and he felt the room swimming.

But he kept his feet, though it took everything

he had. He knew that if he went down, Gooden would be at him with his heavy boots. Then his head cleared as Gooden slammed a left and a right, hitting him on the shoulder and his left bicep. He retaliated by slamming a left hook to Gooden's neck, followed by a long, overhand right that landed on the big man's forehead and clearly stunned him.

Then Gooden charged, grabbing him around the waist and backheeling him. Both fell to the floor, and Slocum for a moment had the wind knocked out of him. But he didn't stop struggling. Gooden was trying to gouge his eyes with his thumbs and was biting Slocum's neck.

Slocum drove his thumb into his opponent's ear, forcing the big man's head back, then twisted and slammed his fist into Gooden's ribs, close to his spine. The big man let out a gasp of pain, and his grip loosened. Slocum broke free and was up on his feet. His opponent rose with the leg of a broken chair, on which both had fallen, in his hand. He swung. Slocum ducked, feinted with his left, bobbed and weaved his body, then brought over a left hook to the big man's rib cage, followed by a smashing overhand right to the jaw, and another left hook to the jaw. And Bart Gooden was out before he hit the floor.

"Christ!" The word broke softly into the scene as all stared at the defeated gladiator who was knocked out, dead to the world, though still breathing after a fashion.

"Jesus," said someone.

Elihu Lincoln Thong wasted not a moment.

"You men get him over onto that bedroll there.

Me and Mister Slocum here got some business to talk over. You hear me now?" And looked at Slocum for backing.

"Hustle it," Slocum said. "You got any other visitors around?"

Nobody said a word.

"That be the size of it then," Elihu said. "I will be showin' Mister Slocum around the place here. You . . ." He nodded at one of the men. "You get Cookie to rustle us some java and biscuits. Hear?" He turned to Slocum. "You want more, do you?"

Slocum shook his head.

"We can take a look about then," Elihu said. " 'less you already seen the outfit, which I don't figger you have."

"You figgered right," Slocum said. "But let's get around some of that arbuckle and biscuits. I worked up a appetite with that feller." He nodded in the direction of Bart Gooden, who was beginning to stir. "Anyway, I have been wanting to talk with you. So it's good you're here. I didn't know you were with this lot."

"I ain't. I have done some work for Undershaft and some for Gooden just like now and again. Keep my hand in. And I know how Undershaft wants you to work with him."

"You recommend it, do you?"

"Wisht you hadn't ast me that question," Elihu said.

"I got your answer, mister."

"He is due out here if you want to stick around. I could ask you why you come by."

"Wanted to check the place. I been hearing some talk about gold. And, well, I'm not looking for the yellow stuff myself, but I am wondering why some-body tried to set fire to Dolly Dolores VanDam's outfit just recently."

"Think you be making a mistake not to throw in with himself," Thong was saying as they nursed their mugs of coffee and smoked. They had left Gooden in the cabin as he had started to come to, and walked out to find Cookie and some biscuits and strong coffee. The men standing around looked at them casually, careful almost to an extreme. The news of how John Slocum had handled their leader had spread quickly. The whole outfit was charged, and in fact Slocum was thinking it might be wise to pull out while he was up on the game. For sure, Bart Gooden wasn't going to take that beating lying down. Slocum knew he could expect a gang-beating or a bullet in the back.

"I know you're thinking of hauling out," his com-panion said, leaning forward and reading his face. " 'ceptin' you got a kind of protection that I figger is stronger than anything Gooden would try on you."

"You mean Undershaft."

"I do. He wants you for his operation. Not only on account of you know how to handle yerself, handle men, get things done, but mostly on account of you got a good record. People trust you. A man knows where he stands with John Slocum. You'd give a good picture to any Undershaft operation—which some sonofabitch like Gooden don't."

"What about yourself?" Slocum asked. "You work with him don't you."

Elihu was shaking his head. "I work with him, not for him. Undershaft don't cotton to that, but

I insist, and he takes it. But, see, I got too many corners for people to handle me. I mean they can't handle you, on account you play it from the chest, see. Me, on the other hand, I play from the pockets." And he lowered one eyelid in a wink, and there was a sly grin on his face.

"Hunh!"

" 'Course, I figure he has got somethin' on you."

"In a way of speakin'."

"But not enough. On the other hand, you'd just as lief he didn't."

"That is so."

"Well, then I reckon you'll play it like it falls. And mind you, I don't allow as that ain't the best hand to have." He chuckled, sizing Slocum with a long look. "I trust you, boy. I wouldn't want to tangle with you, and I'd admire to have you siding me."

"What about Buck Charles?"

"Hah! He is the fly in the ointment. I wouldn't trust Charles far as I can spit gold."

They were silent a moment now as they had started to amble along, having finished their coffee and sourdough biscuits.

"He is working for Undershaft?"

"Can you tell me somebody who isn't?"

"Tell me about the ranchers up on the northern range, the outfits next to Dolly's DV. I got a notion there's more to it than one of them or more wanting Dolly out of there."

They had come to a thin creek that ran along one side of the canyon, and Slocum stopped and his companion followed suit. Both stood swing-hipped, squinting some into the long rays of the late afternoon sun.

"We better be pulling out 'fore nightfall," Elihu said. "Gooden ain't likely to brace either of us when he's sober, but when he's drunk, and that ain't seldom, he's liable to anything."

"I figure."

"He is letting it sink in now, but tonight he'll hit the path. Undershaft's got a tight bit on him, it has to be figured, but the booze can wipe that out right now."

"Good enough," Slocum said. "We'll leave separate. I've seen enough of this here anyway."

They had been standing down by the barn and the round horse corral, and they looked back toward the cabin.

"Did you see Gooden?" Slocum asked his companion.

"Nope."

"The big bay is gone."

"You reckon . . . ?"

"I do."

"Well, like they say, you better watch yer back-trail."

He had hoped, and his hope came through. She was there. As he rode into the DV, the kitchen door opened, and there she was in a white shirt and a plaid skirt that he'd never seen before.

"I had a feeling you might show up," she said. "Had that feeling all day."

"I had it too," he said, smiling quietly at her.

He dismounted, and they stood facing each other.

"Any trouble? Any visitors?"

"No trouble. No visitors."

"Dolly home?"

"She's riding up along the north creek. Matter of fact, she just left a few minutes ago."

"I take it she'll be gone a while."

"What are you getting at, Mister Slocum?"

He already had his arms around her, and their bodies were pressed together. Now her arms slid around his neck as he bent to kiss her on the mouth. Her lips were warm, soft, and now they opened as his tongue felt into her mouth.

"We'd better get inside," she said into her ear, as he thrust his rigid member between her legs.

Inside, she locked the door and in a moment they were on her bed.

"My God, how I want you . . ." Her words tickled his ear, and his erection drove at her.

Swiftly, they were naked, and she was lying on her back with her legs open, receiving his hard member with a gasp of joy.

"I've wanted you so . . ."

"Me too," he said while his hands explored all over her body, slowly, softly. And then, entering her surely with total welcome from her soaking orifice, he rode her slowly, deeply, probing, exploring as his member grew even larger, harder, more commanding with each stroke, as she received and gave thrust for thrust, wrapping her legs around him as now their tempo increased, riding, wiggling in utter ecstacy as they explored, discovered, and at last in the exquisite culmination, found each other as they came, their fluids mixing, their bodies sealed together as they thrust and wove their passion into something unbelievable, something miraculous and endless in their total bliss.

• • •

He began to feel it long before he actually heard the word. He wasn't even within sight of Hardtown. The word was with him, in him, almost *was* him as he rode the Appaloosa at a canter across the long, flat plain and then walked him up the long slope that brought him to the line of spruce and pine and the ridge looking down the other side to the town. It grew stronger as he got closer, until at last he heard the actual word coined on a human tongue. "Gold!"

It was in the livery with the old hostler, in the street with the crowd of people, some of whom he could see had just bought shovels. But it was not yet a roar, a panic, a charging into the attack to find it, dig it, pan it, get it! It hadn't yet consumed the town. It was still a question, latent yet in a sense more powerful than if it had been openly expressed and accepted as a hard fact. "Yes sir, there is indeed gold in them hills. Step this way!" No, it was not yet a panic, a roaring avalanche which would obliterate all with absolutely equal ferocity.

And John Slocum knew it was a fake. Knew it like he knew the bruise on the side of his face where Bart Gooden had landed a lead wallop. Knew it was fake, because it had to be.

The question was why? And who? Who had started it? Who was pumping all that excitement?

It was an excitement, yes, but there was still a wariness about it. People hadn't gone beyond that point of rational thought where they would forget any possibility of reason and good sense and would simply fall into hysteria.

He had stopped at the Trail Cafe for coffee and grub. Not that he was all that hungry, but he did want to think things out a bit. Needed to. Somebody—and it pointed to Undershaft—wanted something. What? Well, Dolly Dolores's DV outfit, for one thing, and likely the neighbors too, for he'd heard that the squeeze was being put on them. Cattle had been rustled, horses stolen. And someone, some eastern combine had wanted to buy up Torgerson's place and his immediate neighbor's and probably the DV as well. Even though it was actually Undershaft who had made the offer to Dolly Dolores, it made sense that he, or someone behind him, if indeed there was anyone higher than himself, wanted that whole big section near Carter Mountain. In fact, Elihu Thong had mentioned something to that effect when they'd gotten together out at Prairie Dog.

Further, there was all the business about Undershaft wanting himself to work for him. Why? The man had it rolling for him two ways from the jack. Why then did he need a fake gold strike? Or was it fake? Maybe there really was gold. Yet, no one had hit town with the yellow on him. It was all rumor thus far, at least so far as Slocum could tell it. Then he found himself wondering about Elihu Thong. Lawyer, he was. Well, that figured. A man like Undershaft would need a lawyer, would have even more than one, more than likely, helping him with all his business.

Hardtown looked to be a town with empty pockets and no prospects for anything better. Was this why Undershaft had picked the place? Why he'd put Buck Charles in the sheriff's job, why he had Elihu

Thong at hand to deal with the public? Why he wanted himself to whipsaw the operation?

But he had Gooden. Gooden could be trouble. The man couldn't be trusted.

Then he ran into Elihu Thong in The Best Time.

"Figured you were still out of town," Slocum said, as Thong nodded to the chair across the table from where he was sitting with his glass of beer.

"Came in especially to see you, my lad."

"Undershaft sent you?"

Elihu nodded. "He did."

"What does he want? Don't tell me. I can guess."

Thong took out a cigar and lighted it before answering. Slocum had declined his offer of a smoke and now waited for an answer to his question about Undershaft.

"He wants you," Elihu Thong said. "And he said that you can name your own price."

"I already have named my price. He knows that, and you know it."

"He wants you to run his whole operation—everything."

"Everything?"

"That includes his new stamp mill."

"What's he doing with a stamp mill?"

"You can guess. It's down at Two Mile Canyon," Elihu went on. "Listen to this. Undershaft has a man named File running the place, but the man can't be trusted. That is, he can't be trusted to do Undershaft's kind of work."

"That's what I would imagine," Slocum said. "He ain't *dis*honest enough!" And they both had a chuckle at that.

But now Slocum was listening more carefully to

Elihu. He had caught something in the man's voice, something that he hadn't heard before.

Elihu laid his cigar on the edge of the round table and leaned forward, his eyes sweeping their immediate environment for eager ears, probing eyes.

His voice had a new tone to it; indeed, Slocum caught a new vibration, as though there was something newly charged in the man. It puzzled him for a moment, and then he caught it. Thong was afraid.

"Slocum, I am worried. I don't mind tellin' it to you. I'm concerned."

And Slocum could see that indeed it was so. The man had lost color in his face, and there was even a slight shaking of his hands.

"What's he doing with a stamp mill?" Slocum asked. "That's what puzzles me. There isn't enough gold or silver around this part of the country to cover a statue of a blue jay." And he was wondering: was Thong just worried, concerned, or was he scared? For a minute, Slocum had thought the man was frightened, but he knew better. He knew Thong's type. He was droll, light-hearted, but also dead serious, and what was more, dependable. And then he caught it; the man was acting.

"Slocum, I need your help. I'm a United States Marshal. Now, I won't show you my credentials here in public, but I will later. Just listen to me. I want you to pretend we're having an argument. I don't want it to look like we're getting along. You understand? You agree?"

"Where you a marshal from?" Slocum asked.

"Chicago."

"You know a man named Clyde Fillmore?"

"Never heard of him."

"What about Don Stevenson?"

"Never heard of him."

"What about Jim Trenton?"

"I know Jim."

Slocum grinned.

"Passed it, huh?" said Elihu wryly.

"You already passed it before I questioned you," Slocum said. "That questioning was more for me than you."

"That's a good way to look at it."

"Tell me about the stamp mill."

Elihu sniffed, then looked down at his thumbnail. "See, there's a lot of action going on around Peterborough."

"I'm not surprised. It's a big strike I've been told."

"Stagecoaches, trains, people, anything and any way the night riders get it coming and going. And it's mostly gold they're pulling."

"I get you. So the question is how to get rid of it without attracting attention."

"You got it."

"The stamp mill. And, I take it, a reduction plant."

"It was like rolling off a log. The gang robbed right and left—at will, as they say in the newspapers. The boys at the stamp mill on Two Mile Canyon began to produce bullion. At first only a bar a month came out, but by the middle of last year the mill was producing six to eight bars a month. Well, no need to go into more detail. The stamp mill, as you can see, was a perfect cover for the stage and train robbers so they could get rid of their ore—they had simply mined it."

"Neat." Slocum took a short pull at his drink, remembering his role of casual conversation with a casual acquaintance. For he knew they were being watched.

"Question is, what is Undershaft doing here in Hardtown?" Saying those words, Thong lifted his eyebrows, pursed his lips, and looked engagingly into the middle distance.

"There being no gold or silver here."

"Right."

"Except that now there is, as the rumors have it."

"Right."

Slocum's forefinger touched the side of his glass. "Are you saying that Undershaft whipsawed that operation in Peterborough and Two Mile Canyon."

"That he did."

"And now he's here in Hardtown," Slocum said, adding it carefully as he tapped his middle finger on the tabletop for each point. "Here in Hardtown, but with no gold. Yet putting out the rumor, through action more than words, that there is gold."

Elihu spread his hands, palms up. "You got a notion?"

"I think so." Slocum leaned forward. "Why would a man spread a story, or incite rumor at any rate, that there is or might be gold where obviously there is not?"

"That's the whole point, dammit! I am stumped!" And Elihu ran his fingers along the top of the table, making a design in the liquid that had sweated off the glass he'd been holding, and then leaned back with his eyes firmly on Slocum. "You got an answer? Looks to me like you do, by golly."

"I believe so. Undershaft isn't looking for gold; he's looking for people who are looking for gold."

"That's got to be it."

"The rumor will bring everyone into his net, where he or his agents will sell claims, but without anyone making the statement that there is actually gold. It will be rumor, supposition, wish, hope, however you want to name it, but it will never, never, never be stated that there is in fact gold!"

"The rubes will dig themselves into it," said Elihu. "You have got it, my friend." He sniffed. "And that, of course, is why he wants you as a front."

"And that's why he's got you with him."

"Yes, he figures I'm as crooked as himself. Which is why I've been playing along."

"I've a notion he might be playing some other game, though I wouldn't be so sure he doesn't know you're from Chicago. Because, you are good cover for him. 'Why, I have a law officer working with me.' Like that."

"I'd thought of that," Elihu allowed. "On account of Undershaft is one smart sonofabitch. The man is no dumbbell!"

"Thing is, what's Undershaft really after?"

"That's it." Elihu looked down at his hands, wagging his head slowly from side to side.

"You don't know?" Slocum said. And he felt the change in atmosphere in the barroom. He could feel the eyes on him and didn't feel too good about his back to the swinging doors, though he had the mirror.

With his eyes still on Elihu Lincoln Thong, he

managed to take in the figure in the mirror behind the bar, the man that had just walked in through the swinging doors.

Suddenly, he realized that while he had taken his seat facing the mirror intentionally, knowing his back would be to the door, it had been Elihu Thong who had waved him to the seat. And he'd had the distinct feeling that the man had been expecting him. More than just expecting—that he had known he was coming there.

It was as if by a signal with his own thought that right then as the realization struck him, the barroom fell silent.

"He wants the railroad, doesn't he?" Slocum asked Elihu Lincoln Thong. "That's why he wants all the people here—so the count is high. Simple isn't it . . ." His eyes had not left Bart Gooden's image in the big mirror for an instant, nor had they left Elihu Thong.

"Slocum!"

And he had half risen, throwing his chair straight back at the man who had called him, then whirling, ducking, and falling onto his back, he shot Bart Gooden right through his neck. And still rolling, feeling the smack of a bullet as it plowed into the barroom floor inches from his head, and another tugging his sleeve, he shot Elihu Lincoln Thong right in his gut.

He was up on his feet then, ready for any more backup, but the room was silent as a church during mass.

Finally someone said, "Holy Mother of God!" The words were more whisper than actual sound. But all must have heard them.

"Them two didn't have a chance," an old swamper mumbled to someone in the back of the room. "Never seen lightnin' like in that man there," the voice went on.

Then a strange voice broke the silence.

"Are you John Slocum, mister?" The words were spoken, very quietly and with respect, from somewhere around the middle of the room.

Slocum's voice was even more quiet and surely more steady. "That's my name, mister. But before I was John Slocum I was me, and I reckon that's who I am right now, and who I'll be when I die. Me."

And that was what he told Sally McQuarie when he saw her later that day, that he was simply himself.

"When you've got yourself, you don't really need anything else," he said.

"I see." She smiled up at him, after they had just finished their second love-making. "But what about Mister Undershaft and the railroad and all that?"

"He won't be able to pull that now. It was a mighty big bluff, about the biggest I've ever run into, and I was almost fooled by Thong."

"How did you know he was lying to you?" she asked. And he wondered if she really wanted to know or was just being nice to get onto the next moment more quickly.

"I asked him if he knew three different people in the Chicago marshal's office. The first two he said no he didn't, and the third he said he did."

"Well, what was wrong with that? Wasn't there such a person?"

"Oh yes, only his name is Tim not Jim. And I made a very clear pronunciation on purpose. Besides, the Chicago office moved about a year ago."

"Mister Slocum?"

He looked down into her large brown eyes. "Yes, young lady."

"All that is very interesting, sir. But I—uh . . ."

"I hear you," he said, closing her mouth with his as her arms circled his neck and shoulders, her legs opened and he mounted her smoothly and with the greatest joy.

"How long do we have, John?" she whispered in his ear.

"Forever, plus right now."

SPECIAL PREVIEW!

Award-winning author Bill Gulick presents his epic trilogy of the American West, the magnificent story of two brothers, Indian and white man, bound by blood and divided by destiny. . . .

Northwest Destiny

This classic saga includes *Distant Trails*, *Gathering Storm*, and *River's End*.

Here is a special excerpt from book one, DISTANT TRAILS—available from Jove books. . . .

For the last hundred yards of the stalk, neither man had spoken—not even in whispers—but communicated by signs as they always did when hunting meat to fill hungry bellies. Two steps ahead, George Drewyer, the man recognized to be the best hunter in the Lewis and Clark party, sank down on his right knee, froze, and peered intently through the glistening wet bushes and dangling evergreen tree limbs toward the animal grazing in the clearing. Identifying it, he turned, using his hands swiftly and graphically to tell the younger, less experienced hunter, Matt Crane, the nature of the animal he had seen and how he meant to approach and kill it.

Not a deer, his hands said. Not an elk. Just a stray Indian horse—with no Indians in sight. He'd move up on it from downwind, his hands said, until he got into sure-kill range, then he'd put a ball from his long rifle into its head. What he expected Matt to do was follow a couple of steps behind and a few feet off to the right, stopping when he stopped, aiming when he aimed, but firing only if the actions of the horse clearly showed that Drewyer's ball had missed.

Matt signed that he understood. Turning back toward the clearing, George Drewyer began his final stalk.

Underfoot, the leaf mold and fallen pine needles formed a yielding carpet beneath the scattered clumps of bushes and thick stands of pines, which here on the western slope of the Bitter Root Mountains were broader in girth and taller than the skinny lodgepole and larch found on the higher reaches of the Lolo Trail. Half a day's travel behind, the other thirty-two members of the party still were struggling in foot-deep snow over slick rocks, steep slides, and tangles of down timber treacherous as logjams, as they sought the headwaters of the Columbia and the final segment of their journey to the Pacific Ocean.

It had been four days since the men had eaten meat, Matt knew, being forced to sustain themselves on the detested army ration called "portable soup," a grayish brown jelly that looked like a mixture of pulverized wood duff and dried dung, tasted like iron filings, and even when flavored with meat drippings and dissolved in hot water satisfied the belly no more than a swallow of air. Nor had the last solid food been much, for the foal butchered at Colt-Killed Creek had been dropped by its dam only a few months ago; though its meat was tender enough, most of its growth had gone into muscle and bone, its immature carcass making skimpy portions when distributed among such a large party of famished men.

With September only half gone, winter had already come to the seven-thousand-foot-high backbone of the continent a week's travel behind. All the game that the old Shoshone guide, Toby, had told them usually was to be found in the high meadows at this time of year had moved down to lower levels. Desperate for food, Captain William Clark had sent George Drewyer and Matt Crane scouting ahead for meat, judging that two men traveling afoot and unencumbered would stand a much better chance of finding game than the main party with its thirty-odd men and twenty-nine heavily laden horses. As he usually did, Drewyer had found game of a sort, weighed the risk of rousing the hostility of its Indian owner against the need of the party for food, and decided that hunger recognized no property rights.

In the drizzling cold rain, the coat of the grazing horse glistened like polished metal. It would be around four years old, Matt guessed, a brown and white paint, well muscled, sleek, alert. If this were a typical Nez Perce horse, he could well believe what the Shoshone chief, Cameahwait, had told Captain Clark—that the finest horses to be found in this part of the country were those raised by the Shoshones' mortal enemies, the Nez Perces. Viewing such a handsome animal cropping bluegrass on a Missouri hillside eighteen months ago, Matt Crane would have itched to rope, saddle, and ride it, testing its speed, wind, and spirit. Now all he itched to do was kill and eat it.

Twenty paces away from the horse, which still was grazing placidly, George Drewyer stopped, knelt behind a fallen tree, soundlessly rested the barrel of his long rifle on its trunk, and took careful aim. Two steps to his right, Matt Crane did the same. After what seemed an agonizingly long period of time, during which Matt held his breath, Drewyer's rifle barked. Without movement or sound, the paint horse sank to the ground, dead— Matt was sure—before its body touched the sodden earth.

"Watch it!" Drewyer murmured, swiftly reversing his rifle, swabbing out its barrel with the ramrod, expertly reloading it with patched and greased lead ball, wiping flint and firing hammer clean, then opening the pan and pouring in a carefully measured charge while he protected it from the drizzle with the tree trunk and his body.

Keeping his own rifle sighted on the fallen horse, Matt held his position without moving or speaking, as George Drewyer had taught him to do, until the swarthy, dark-eyed hunter had reloaded his weapon and risen to one knee. Peering first at the still animal, then moving his searching gaze around the clearing, Drewyer tested the immediate environment with all his senses—sight, sound, smell, and his innate hunter's instinct—for a full minute before he at last nodded in satisfaction.

"A bunch-quitter, likely. Least there's no herd nor herders around. Think you can skin it, preacher boy?"

"Sure. You want it quartered, with the innards saved in the hide?"

"Just like we'd do with an elk. Save everything but the hoofs and whinny. Get at it, while I snoop around for Injun sign. The Nez Perces will be friendly, the captains say, but I'd as soon not meet the Injun that owned that horse till its head and hide are out of sight."

While George Drewyer circled the clearing and prowled through the timber beyond, Matt Crane went to the dead horse, unsheathed his butcher knife, skillfully made the cuts needed to strip off the hide, and gutted and dissected the animal. Returning from his scout, Drewyer hunkered down beside him, quickly boned out as large a packet of choice cuts as he could conveniently carry, wrapped them in a piece of hide, and loaded the still-warm meat into the empty canvas backpack he had brought along for that purpose.

"It ain't likely the men'll get this far by dark," he said, "so I'll take 'em a taste to ease their bellies for the night. Can you make out alone till tomorrow noon?"

"Yes."

"From what I seen, the timber thins out a mile or so ahead. Seems to be a kind of open, marshy prairie beyond, which is where the Nez Perces come this time of year to dig roots, Toby says. Drag the head and hide back in the bushes out of sight. Cut the meat up into pieces you can spit and broil, then build a fire and start it cooking. If the smoke and smell brings Injun company, give 'em the peace sign, invite 'em to sit and eat, and tell 'em a big party of white men will be coming down the trail tomorrow. You got all that, preacher boy?"

"Yes."

"Good. Give me a hand with this pack and I'll be on my way." Slipping his arms through the straps and securing the pad that transferred a portion of the weight to his forehead, Drewyer got to his feet while Matt Crane eased the load. Grinning, Drewyer squeezed his shoulder. "Remind me to quit calling you preacher boy, will you, Matt? You've learned a lot since you left home."

"I've had a good teacher."

"That you have! Take care."

Left alone in the whispering silence of the forest and the cold, mistlike rain, Matt Crane dragged the severed head and hide into a clump of nearby bushes. Taking his hatchet, he searched for and found enough resinous wood, bark, and dry duff to catch the spark from his flint and steel. As the fire grew in the narrow trench he had dug for it, he cut forked sticks, placed pieces of green aspen limbs horizontally across them, sliced the meat into strips, and started it to broiling. The smell of juice dripping into the fire made his belly churn with hunger, tempting him to do what Touissant Charbonneau, the party's French-Canadian interpreter, did when fresh-killed game was brought into camp—seize a hunk and gobble it down hot, raw, and bloody. But he did not, preferring to endure the piercing hunger pangs just a little longer in exchange for the greater pleasure of savoring his first bite of well-cooked meat.

Cutting more wood for the fire, he hoped George Drewyer would stop calling him "preacher boy." Since at twenty he was one of the youngest members of the party and his father, the Reverend Peter Crane, was a Presbyterian minister in St. Louis, it had been natural enough for the older men to call him "the preacher's boy" at first. Among a less disciplined band, he would have been forced to endure a good deal of hoorawing and would have been the butt of many practical jokes. But the no-nonsense military leadership of the two captains put strict limits on that sort of thing.

Why Drewyer—who'd been raised a Catholic, could barely read and write, and had no peer as an outdoorsman—should have made Matt his protégé, Matt himself could not guess. Maybe because he was malleable, did what he was told to do, and never backed off from hard work. Maybe because he listened more than he talked. Or maybe because he was having the adventure of his life and showed it. Whatever the reason, their relationship was good. It would be even better, Matt mused, if Drewyer would drop the "preacher boy" thing and simply call him by name.

While butchering the horse, Matt noticed that it had been gelded as a colt. According to George Drewyer, the Nez Perces were one of the few Western Indian tribes that practiced selective breeding, thus the high quality of their horses. From the way Chief Cameahwait had acted, a state of war existed between the Shoshones and the Nez Perces, so the first contact between the Lewis and Clark party—which had passed through Shoshone country—and the Nez Perces was going to be fraught with danger. Aware of the fact that he might make the first contact, Matt Crane felt both uneasy and proud. Leaving him alone in this area showed the confidence Drewyer had in him. But his aloneness made him feel a little spooky.

With the afternoon only half gone and nothing to do but tend the fire, Matt stashed his blanket roll under a tree out of the wet, picked up his rifle, and curiously studied the surrounding forest. There was no discernible wind, but vagrant currents of air stirred, bringing to his nostrils the smell of wood smoke, of crushed pine needles, of damp leaf mold, of burnt black powder. As he moved across the clearing toward a three-foot-wide stream gurgling down the slope, he scowled, suddenly realizing that the burnt black powder smell could not have lingered behind this long. Nor would it have gotten stronger, as this smell was doing the nearer he came to the stream. Now he identified it beyond question.

Sulfur! There must be a mineral-impregnated hot spring nearby, similar to the hot springs near Traveler's Rest at the eastern foot of Lolo Pass, where the cold, weary members of the party had eased their aches and pains in warm, soothing pools. What he wouldn't give for a hot bath right now!

At the edge of the stream, he knelt, dipping his hand into the water. It was warm. Cupping his palm, he tasted it, finding it strongly sulfurous. If this were like the stream on the other side of the mountains, he mused, there would be one or more scalding, heavily impregnated springs issuing from old volcanic rocks higher up the slope, their waters diluted by colder side rivulets joining the main stream, making it simply a matter of exploration to find water temperature and a chemical content best suited to the need of a cold, tired body. The prospect intrigued him.

Visually checking the meat broiling over the fire, he judged it could do without tending for an hour or so. Thick though the forest cover was along the sides of the stream, he would run no risk of getting lost, for following the stream downhill would bring him back to the clearing. Time enough then to cut limbs for a lean-to and rig a shelter for the night.

Sometimes wading in the increasingly warm waters of the stream, sometimes on its bush-bordered bank, he followed its windings uphill for half a mile before he found what he was looking for: a pool ten feet long and half as wide, eroded in smooth basalt, ranging in depth from one to four feet. Testing the temperature of its water, he found it just right—hot but not unbearably so, the sulfur smell strong but not unpleasant. Leaning his rifle against a tree trunk, he took off his limp, shapeless red felt hat, pulled his thin moccasins off his bruised and swollen feet, waded into the pool, and gasped with sensual pleasure as the heat of the water spread upward.

Since his fringed buckskin jacket and woolen trousers already were soaking wet from the cold rain, he kept them on as he first sank to a sitting position, then stretched out full length on his back, with only his head above water. After a time, he roused himself long enough to strip the jacket off over his head and pull the trousers down over his ankles. Tossing them into a clump of bushes near his rifle, hat, and moccasins, he lay back in the soothing water, naked, warm, and comfortable for the first time since Traveler's Rest.

Drowsily, his eyes closed. He slept . . .

The sound that awakened him some time later could have been made by a deer moving down to drink from the pool just upstream from where he lay. It could have been made by a beaver searching for a choice willow sapling to cut down. It could

have been made by a bobcat, a bear, or a cougar.
But as consciousness returned to him, as he heard
the sound and attempted to identify it, his intel-
ligence rejected each possibility that occurred to
him the moment it crossed his mind—for one lucid
reason.

Animals did not sing. And whatever this intrud-
er into his state of tranquillity might be, it was
singing.

Though the words were not recognizable, they
had an Indian sound, unmistakably conveying the
message that the singer was at peace with the
world, not self-conscious, and about to indulge in
a very enjoyable act. Turning over on his belly,
Matt crawled to the upper end of the pool, peering
through the screening bushes in the direction from
which the singing sound was coming. The light was
poor. Even so, it was good enough for him to make
out the figure of a girl, standing in profile not
ten feet away, reaching down to the hem of her
buckskin skirt, lifting it, and pulling it up over her
head.

As she tossed the garment aside, she turned,
momentarily facing him. His first thought was *My
God, she's beautiful!* His second: *She's naked!* His
third, *How can I get away from here without being
seen?*

That she was not aware of his presence was
made clear enough by the fact that she still was
crooning her bath-taking song, her gaze intent on
her footing as she stepped gingerly into a pool just
a few yards upstream from the one in which he
lay. Though he had stopped breathing for fear she
would hear the sound, he could not justify leaving

his eyes open for fear she would hear the lids closing. Morally wrong though he knew it was to stare at her, he could not even blink or look away.

She would be around sixteen years old, he judged, her skin light copper in color, her mouth wide and generous, with dimples indenting both cheeks. Her breasts were full but not heavy; her waist was slim, her stomach softly rounded, her hips beginning to broaden with maturity, her legs long and graceful. Watching her sink slowly into the water until only the tips of her breasts and her head were exposed, Matt felt no guilt for continuing to stare at her. Instead he mused, *So that's what a naked woman looks like! Why should I be ashamed to admire such beauty?*

He began breathing again, careful to make no sound. Since the two pools were no more than a dozen feet apart, separated by a thin screen of bushes and a short length of stream, which here made only a faint gurgling noise, he knew that getting out of the water, retrieving his clothes and rifle, and then withdrawing from the vicinity without revealing his presence would require utmost caution. But the attempt must be made, for if one young Indian woman knew of this bathing spot, others must know of it, too, and in all likelihood soon would be coming here to join her.

He could well imagine his treatment at their hands, if found. Time and again recently the two captains had warned members of the party that Western Indians such as the Shoshones, Flatheads, and Nez Perces had a far higher standard of morality than did the Mandans, with whom the party had wintered, who would gladly sell the favor of wives and daughters for a handful of beads, a piece of bright cloth, or a cheap trade knife, and cheerfully provide shelter and bed for the act.

Moving with infinite care, he half floated, half crawled to the lower right-hand edge of the pool, where he had left his rifle and clothes. The Indian girl still was singing. The bank was steep and slick. Standing up, he took hold of a sturdy-feeling, thumb-thick sapling rooted near the edge of the bank, cautiously tested it, and judged it secure. Pulling himself out of the pool, he started to take a step, slipped, and tried to save himself by grabbing the sapling with both hands.

The full weight of his body proved too much for its root system. Torn out of the wet earth, it no longer supported him. As he fell backward into the pool, he gave an involuntary cry of disgust.

"Oh, shit!"

Underwater, his mouth, nose, and eyes filled as he struggled to turn over and regain his footing. When he did so, he immediately became aware of the fact that the girl had stopped singing. Choking, coughing up water, half-blinded, and completely disoriented, he floundered out of the pool toward where he thought his clothes and rifle were. Seeing a garment draped over a bush, he grabbed it, realized it was not his, hastily turned away, and blundered squarely into a wet, naked body.

To save themselves from falling, both he and the Indian girl clung to each other momentarily. She began screaming. Hastily he let her go. Still screaming and staring at him with terror-stricken eyes, she snatched her dress off the bush and held it so that it covered her. Finding his own clothes, he held them in front of his body, trying to calm the girl by making the sign for "friend," "white man," and "peace," while urgently saying:

"*Ta-ba-bone,* you understand? *Suyapo!* I went to sleep, you see, and had no idea you were around . . ."

Suddenly her screaming stopped. Not because of his words or hand signs, Matt feared, but because of the appearance of an Indian man who had pushed through the bushes and now stood beside her. He was dressed in beaded, fringed buckskins, was stocky, slightly bowlegged, a few inches shorter than Matt but more muscular and heavier, a man in his middle twenties, with high cheekbones and a firm jawline. He shot a guttural question at the girl, to which she replied in a rapid babble of words. His dark brown eyes blazed with anger. Drawing a glittering knife out of its sheath, he motioned the girl to step aside, and moved toward Matt menacingly.

Backing away, Matt thought frantically, *Captain Clark is not going to like this at all. And if that Indian does what it looks like he means to do with that knife, I'm not going to like it, either . . .*